PENGUIN BOOKS

RIVERRUN

Danton Remoto is a Professor of Creative Writing and Head of School, English, at the University of Nottingham Malaysia. He was educated at Ateneo de Manila University, University of Stirling, University of the Philippines, and Rutgers University. He has received fellowships and honours from the Asian Scholarship Foundation, British Council, Fulbright Foundation, and the Don Carlos Palanca Awards for Literature, among others. The Writers' Union of the Philippines gave him a National Achievement Award in Literature (Gawad Balagtas sa Panitikan) in 2015. He was a Fellow at the Cambridge Conference on Contemporary Literature at Downing College, Cambridge University and the Bread Loaf Writers' Conference at Middlebury College, Vermont. He has published a book of short fiction, three books of poems, and five books of non-fiction, all written originally in English. His body of work is cited in *The Routledge Concise History of Southeast Asian Writing in English*, *The Encyclopedia of Postcolonial Literature*, and *The Oxford Research Encyclopedia of Literature*.

D0911477

ADVANCE PRAISE FOR THE BOOK

"I am a fan of the works of Danton Remoto."

Junot Diaz
Winner of the Pulitzer Prize and the National
Book Critics Circle Award for the novel,
The Brief Wondrous Life of Oscar Wao

"Set during the Marcos years, rich in childhood memories of local customs, myths and food. A compelling and entertaining coming-of-age memoir about a Filipino young man's discovery of his sexuality."

Suchen Christine Lim
Winner of the Singapore Literature Prize
and the South East Asia Write Award

"Danton Remoto is an accomplished writer whose fiction is marked by elegant and intense language. I am also impressed with the social concern in his writing, wrought well in images so clear it is like seeing pebbles resting at the bottom of a pond."

Sir Stephen Spender
Winner of the Golden PEN Award
Appointed as United States Poet Laureate

"Danton Remoto is one of the Philippines' best writers."

The Age of Melbourne

"The exquisite writings of Danton Remoto form part of the Philippines' new heart."

James Hamilton-Paterson
Winner of the Whitbread Award for the Novel, UK
Author of the acclaimed novel, *Cooking with Fernet Branca*

"The fiction of Danton Remoto is part of South East Asia's literature of dissent. He writes with clarity and compassion about growing up in a region that is in never-ending ferment."

Asiaweek Magazine

"Danton Remoto is such a wonderful writer. In *Riverrun: A Novel*, he writes about the tropical Catholic magic that saves and destroys."

Tiphanie Yanique
Winner of the American Academy of Arts and
Letters Award and the Flaherty Dunnan Prize
for the novel, *Land of Love and Drowning*

"*Riverrun: A Novel* points to a new direction for South East Asian writing in English. It is intimately personal yet utterly political, the prose polished like marble, and his profound reflections are caught in memory's cold eye. This book will fly!"

Nick Joaquin
Winner, Ramon Magsaysay Award for
Literature (Asia's Nobel Prize) National
Artist for Literature, the Philippines

"*Riverrun: A Novel* is a swift, tender, sometimes rueful *bildungsroman* about a gay youth exploring the contours of his desires and the limits of his potential. The chapters traipse lightly but thoughtfully through episodes of a life, with glancing social commentary and heartfelt recollections of defining relationships."

Cyril Wong
Winner of the Singapore Literature Prize

"I like the passion and the intensity in the fiction of Danton Remoto. Most importantly, I like the fact that he writes with heart—which is the only way to write."

Bienvenido N. Santos
Winner of the American Book Award for
Scent of Apples and Other Stories Winner of
the South East Asia Write Award

"I only have admiration for the fiction of Danton Remoto. The vessel of form and the fluid of content are fused in one organic whole in his works."

NVM Gonzalez
National Artist for Literature, the Philippines
Winner of the Republic Cultural Heritage Award
for the novel, *The Bamboo Dancers*

"One of the best writers of his generation. His words have wings."

"Danton Remoto's fiction is full of marvels. Deep insights spring out at the reader from harmless-looking paragraph corners, keen observations startle the reader into looking at everyday reality with more alert eyes, and unexpected words make the prose exciting. Quite simply, he is one of Asia's best writers."

"Danton Remoto is an outrageously good writer. He writes with substance and style, and he knows history—the context that shapes fiction—like the lines on the palm of his hand."

"To read *Riverrun, A Novel* is to be beguiled by a storyteller at the height of his powers. Danton Remoto weaves the personal with the political, in prose that is deeply evocative, deliciously acid, and unflinchingly truthful."

"Danton Remoto writes with clarity and depth. *Riverrun* is a fine and vivid exploration into the human heart. It is also a passionate excoriation of those who have turned the country into a prison house."

"The Ateneo de Manila University has produced some of the best Filipino writers in the last three decades. One of them is Danton Remoto, who writes poetry and prose of the highest order."

Riverrun

A Novel

Danton Remoto

PENGUIN BOOKS

An imprint of Penguin Random House

PENGUIN BOOKS

USA | Canada | UK | Ireland | Australia
New Zealand | India | South Africa | China | Southeast Asia

Penguin Books is part of the Penguin Random House group of companies
whose addresses can be found at global.penguinrandomhouse.com

Published by Penguin Random House SEA Pte Ltd
9, Changi South Street 3, Level 08-01,
Singapore 486361

Penguin
Random House
SEA

First published in Penguin Books by Penguin Random House SEA 2020

ISBN 9789814882866

Typeset in Adobe Garamond Pro by Manipal Technologies Limited, Manipal
Printed at Markono Print Media Pte Ltd, Singapore

www.penguin.sg

For my father, Francisco Onrubia Remoto
(4 June 1933–19 October 2009)
and
my mother, Lilia Relato Remoto
(10 March 1932–19 November 2009)

Contents

Part 2: The Country of Dreams

Acknowledgments

Extracts from this work have been published in the following magazines and journals: *Ani, Heights, Manila Chronicle, The Manila Times, Metro Magazine Fiction Issue, National Midweek, Philippines Free Press, Philippines Graphic, Philippine STAR, Sunday Inquirer Magazine Summer Reading Issue, The Blithe House Quarterly* (U.S.A.), and www.abs-cbnnews.com.

I would like to thank the following editors for publishing these extracts: Noel Alumit, Gregorio C. Brillantes, Isagani de Castro, Nick Joaquin, Jose F. Lacaba, Millet Mananquil, Malou Mangahas and Thelma San Juan.

'How I Spent My Summer Vacation' was anthologized in *Golden Harvest: Essays in Honour of Fr. Joseph A. Galdon. S.J.*, edited by Edna Zapanta-Manlapaz, Susan Evangelista, et al. Quezon City: Office of Research and Publications, Ateneo de Manila University, 2000.

'Ice Drop' was anthologized in *My Fair Maladies*, edited by Cristina Pantoja Hidalgo. Quezon City: Milflores Publishing, Inc., 2005.

'The Freak Show' was anthologized in *Very Short Stories for Harried Readers*, edited by Vicente Garcia Groyon. Quezon City: Milflores Publishing, Inc., 2007.

'Yes, the Miss Universe!' was published in *Happy Na, Gay Pa* by Danton Remoto. Mandaluyong City: Anvil Publishing, 2015.

In their earlier versions, 'The Kite' won an award at the Philippine Board on Books for Young People Short Story Contest; 'The Heart of Summer' won an award at the *Philippines Free Press* Literary Contest; and 'Wings of Desire' won an award at the *Philippine Graphic* Literary Contest.

The recipe for *kinunut* was based on an entry in *The Coconut Cookery of Bicol* written by Honesto C. General and published by Anvil in 1994. The other recipes were based on entries in *Pulutan: From the Soldiers' Kitchen* by Elmer D. Cruz and Emerson R. Rosales, military officers and gentlemen both. This controversial book, edited by Ellen T. Tordesillas and Yvonne T. Chua and published by Anvil in 2007, was launched with military guards in attendance, for Officers Cruz and Rosales were on trial for the Oakwood Hotel Mutiny in 2003.

I would like to thank the British Council and the International Writers' Fellowship at Hawthornden Castle, Midlothian, Scotland, as well as the Fulbright Scholarship Foundation and the English Department of Rutgers University for the clean, well-lighted places that allowed me to write an early draft of this novel. I would also like to acknowledge the support by the James and Mary Mulvey Fellowship Grant and the University Research Council of Ateneo de Manila University in revising the novel.

My gratitude also goes to the Bread Loaf Writers' Conference 2018 in Middlebury College, Vermont, and to Professor Tiphanie Yanique, a marvellous writer, for sound suggestions on the craft of fiction.

I would like to thank Dr Carol Smith, Rayvi Sunico, Joy Uy-tioco and Lourdes Hernandez Vidal for reading the drafts of this novel and giving suggestions for revision. Finally, I would like to thank Nora Nazerene Abu Bakar, the executive editor at

Penguin Books Southeast Asia, for her deep and abiding faith in my novel; and thanks to my editor, Priyanka Sarkar, for her excellent blue pencil, her kindness and her patience.

The generosity of heart is all theirs but the faults of the book, if not in the stars, are all mine.

And finally, my forever love goes to James, my partner, for reminding me that the most important thing for me is to write.

Part 1

Memory's Clear, White Light

Words

Words. Their shadow and light.

My mother taught me the alphabet even before I joined kindergarten. She would sit beside me, guiding my hand to form the arcs, loops and crosses, the dips and turns of the letters: the alphabets in a whirl of a dance. I would copy on to my lined paper the individual letters and then the words formed by joining one letter with the next, unlocking meanings, pulling them away from each other's loneliness.

One word would join another, turning into a sentence, a whole train of them turning into paragraphs, into pages, into books!

On rainy mornings when I could not leave the house to play in the backyard, I would plump up my pillow and let it stand against the bed's wooden headboard. Then I would pull the string of the lampshade (light, warm like skin) and begin to read. When my book was new, I would open it slowly, slowly, in the middle, then I would bring it closer to my nose. I would inhale the smell of paper and ink, thread and glue, imagine I am inhaling the very fragrances of words. Then I would begin to read.

A world of words, a universe of sorrows and joys. Open sesame, and out tumbled the tales of Scheherazade told in a thousand and one nights (how deliciously frightening to have your life depend on a tale). Alice wandering into the labyrinths of wonder (how the jaw would drop at every episode, turning like the lobes of a seashell). And later, the stories of Bienvenido N. Santos (oh you lovely people, Filipinos in a foreign land, Asian-Hispanic-American, sassy, bright and noisy, the inner melancholy). The poems of Pablo Neruda (my heartbeats run to you like the sea to the shore).

A geography of feelings, then, from the hidden treasures of a cave to the sea shimmering like the roundest of pearls.

The Hitchhiker

'A full moon with no scar shone on the night you were born,' my father said to me as he sat under the shade cast by the star-apple tree in the yard. He was tall and he sat on the *perezosa*, the lazy lounge chair, with his long legs resting on a wooden bench.

I had been pulling out his white hair using a tweezer. Five white hairs meant five centavos. Business was brisk. Fifteen white hairs meant a bottle of RC Cola. I asked him about the small square thing wrapped in layers of old, yellowed cotton, hung on a string and dangling from the ceiling just outside my window.

'That is your umbilical cord,' he answered. 'The doctor, who was my friend, wrapped it in cotton, then gave it for me to hang from our ceiling.'

'Why, Papa?' I asked.

'So you do not wander far from home.'

The cool wind rising seemed to move him to tell more stories.

'It was the night you were born. We still did not have a jeep then, so I was taking the bicycle that night, on my way to the hospital. I was already in front of the huge *balete* tree, its roots like knotted arms, when I felt the bicycle become heavier. It was not an uphill climb, but why did it suddenly feel so heavy?'

By this time, I had stopped probing my father's head for my RC Cola.

'Suddenly I knew that somebody was sitting behind me, on my bicycle. That it was a woman in white, with long black hair streaming in the night, and that she had no face. Only a black void. In my mind I told her to leave. I told her my first child will be born tonight and my wife has been going through labour pains, on and off, in the last two days . . .'

'And then what happened, Papa?' I asked.

'She did let go in the end and so I sped away as quick as lightning. When I reached the hospital, you were just being delivered, bald and red and sticky all over and squealing madly at the world.'

The Magic Box

I was four years old, sleeping soundly on my parents' big and wide bed. One morning, my mother—my slender and beautiful mother—woke me up, brought me to the bathroom where she washed my face, and made me rinse my mouth. When we returned to their room, she said. 'This is the day I told you about. The man with the magic black box will come today.'

She dressed me up. She pulled out my new white, short-sleeved polo shirt from its plastic bag and shook it in the morning air. Against my skin the shirt was crisp and clean. Mama made me wear my new khaki shorts. She buttoned up my shirt and then knotted a green tie under my stiff collar.

'Now, you already look properly dressed,' she said. 'Remember this: when the man stands before his magic black box and disappears under the black cloth, you should give him your widest smile.' I was still groggy from sleep, so I just nodded at her.

Whiteness, there was whiteness everywhere! The walls and ceilings of our house with its French windows. The bark of the pine trees in the yard painted white, as Brigadier General Armando Bautista, the commander of the military airbase, had ordered. And then, when we stepped out of the house, the whitest of sky, whiter than the bond paper that Mama would give me, along with a big box of crayons. From this box, I would take out the crayons one by one, memorizing their colours: blue, yellow and red; violet, orange and green.

The man inside the van had hair as stiff as a toothbrush. He was as big as a cabinet. He asked me to sit down on a wicker chair in the middle of the van. Behind me was a curtain in pale green. Mama was just outside, I kept telling myself. The man then waddled to where the magic black box stood. 'Okay, son, ready?' he asked.

I just nodded, noticing the cracks on his pair of brown shoes.

Then his head disappeared under the black cloth. 'Smile, son,' he said.

I smiled as he began to count. Ready, one, two, three. But at the count of three, I stopped smiling. I just looked at him straight, behind that magic black box, then tilted my head slightly to the right, as if listening to a voice only I could hear.

Now as I look at that first posed shot (thin hair, oblong head, the most piercing eyes), I still find myself listening to a voice coming as if from afar. In vain, I would wait for it would never arrive, and then there would only be the sudden explosion of light.

The Visit

L ike a sneeze it spread amongst my friends, the news that the president would visit our military airbase. Perhaps, drop by would have been a better word. For on that day, with the September sky the colour of lead, the presidential plane landed on the runway stretching from the hangar like a grey tongue. In the horizon loomed the blue Zambales mountain range, including a volcano called Mount Pinatubo that had been dormant for 500 years.

It was a Saturday. Since we had no classes, my friend Luis and I jumped on to our bikes and sped in the direction of the runway. Of course, we should not be seen, so we just crouched on a slope, beneath the coconut trees, and watched the big presidential plane with the tricolour of the flag on its side make a smooth, graceful landing. The stainless-steel door opened, and there was the president, in his crisp off-white Barong Tagalog. The spun pineapple fibres sheathed the body that was still young and firm, the chest of the bemedalled war hero of the country. Youngest mayor, youngest governor, youngest congressman, youngest senator, and now, the youngest president of the country, the so-called pearl of the orient seas.

His eyes seemed to crinkle in the unimaginable heat as he walked down the plane. At the landing he stopped and acknowledged the salute of the generals arrayed before him like penguins. Swift and sharp was his salute, his thumb a small wing beneath the four fingers slanting to the sky. His hair was well-cut, his eyes staring straight ahead, lips pressed together—a face poised forward, as if to the future.

'But the president did not stay long,' Luis complained later, when we were already having soda and biscuits from the commissary. Luis was right. He returned the salute of Brigadier General Armando Bautista. After this, he handed over a sheaf of papers to the brigadier general and exchanged a few words with him. Then, the president turned around and climbed the stairs again. The last thing I saw was his pure, off-white, dazzling barong, before he was swallowed up by the darkness of the plane.

The First Television

Boy, who lived in front of our house, told me one day that they had just bought a television set from Ocampo's Appliance Store on M. Hizon Street in San Fernando. Now he could watch *Casper, the Friendly Ghost, Josie and the Pussycats, Batman and Robin, Spider Man* and *The Flintstones*, yaba-daba-doo, every night.

I took the news as an invitation, so one afternoon, after leaving my blue school bag in the room, I rushed out of the house, past my grandmother who was watering the lawn, on to the street beginning to turn gold from the sunset. I only stopped running when I reached the yard of Boy's house.

I was about to enter through their door when I met his mother, who was just stepping out of the door. Now, Boy's mother was the type who had been immortalized in countless sitcoms, drama shows and even advertisements. In the morning, her hair would be a nest of rollers; in the afternoon her face would be greasy from all that cooking.

'So,' she asked me, shapeless in her faded floral house dress, 'where are you going?'

'To watch TV. Boy said your new TV set was delivered yesterday.'

'Yes, but we're not inviting anybody to watch it,' she said, her thick lips twisting with her words, like the villain in Filipino movies.

11

I was young and stupid, so I just stared at her. She stepped backward, held the doorknob with her left hand and slammed the door shut on my face. I stood there, my feelings in chaos. My ears burnt with a flame I could not see and a great terrible anger began rising within me. It was the kind that would rarely rise from me, but when it came, it exploded with a fury.

I walked down their cemented stairs, grabbed a pebble, no, a rock, and hurled it at their windowpane.

The smashed window looked like the teeth of a shark.

I ran in the gathering dusk, past my grandmother merging with the shadows, into the living room floating with the smell of fried chicken for dinner. I ran right into my room. I locked the door and sat down in the dark.

Then I heard our jeep nosing into the garage and my father's voice. In his wake, a series of voices, then a series of loud knocks on my door.

I braced myself and opened the door. Papa was there, his face cold and impassive. Behind him was Mama's stricken face. And behind her, my grandmother who had just awakened from her late afternoon nap.

Papa grabbed my hand, dragged me to the kitchen, asked me if it was true; I nodded, and clamped my lips. He made me lie down, face flat against the hard, wooden bench. I knew what was coming. Then his leather belt began lashing at my buttocks and the skin of my thighs. Once, twice, thrice. I was just silent, my teeth biting into my lips. I told myself I won't let Papa hear me cry.

Papa said, in between the lashings, that he would not raise a child like me, that I should learn to check my temper and that we could also afford to buy a TV set. I should have asked for one, that he would never be shamed by a woman who never finished elementary school and whose husband was the dumbest trainee in military school, the one in the Philippines, not even the one in Colorado, since this dumbo did not make the cut to study overseas.

All these words were flung at me while his leather belt cut the air, then bit into my skin. After the third lashing, Mama said, 'Stop,' but Papa could not be appeased. And so my grandmother, my old and magnificent grandmother, stood between Papa and me and said in a voice that when I remember it now, still gave me the shivers. She said to Papa, 'If you don't want to stop, then strike me.'

I looked back. Papa's hand froze mid-air, the belt hanging limply, like a sail suddenly without wind. Then he turned his back and walked away. My grandmother went to the bench, gathered me in her arms, and led me slowly back to her room.

My grandmother's room smelt of white flower and the medicinal oil Pak Fah Yeow, which she bought from the Chinese merchants in Binondo, all the way in Manila. She ran her fingers through my hair.

Later in life, my grandmother would return to Albay, to live in the old, wooden house my grandfather had built for her. But I only had to smell white flower or open the small bottle of Pak Fah Yeow, let the soothing smell permeate the air, and I would be back in her room again. Her hand rested on my forehead. Then she ran her fingers through my hair, my small and dark grandmother, the 'ugliest' among her fair-skinned sisters as she had claimed, her voice warm and consoling. Suddenly, I began to sob, a sharp sob that tore at me savagely, now that my father was no longer there to see me. I cried myself into a deep, deep sleep.

It was Papa who woke me up the next morning. He told me in a kind voice to wash my face and take a warm bath, so we could all have breakfast together. He even led me by the hand to the washbasin.

After a breakfast of garlic rice, dried fish and eggs sunny side-up, he brought me to their room. He asked me to stand before him while he sat down and examined my thighs. I knew that they had lines on them, like the tracks of tyres and parts of my skin had turned ashen-grey. He asked me why he gave me a lashing, his voice uncommonly gentle, and I told him about Boy, their TV set, his sea-hag of a mother (although I didn't say 'sea-hag', then: I didn't want another lashing), my anger, the rock smashing the neighbour's window.

He asked me, 'Did you do the right thing?'

I was silent. Of course it was wrong, I wanted to tell him, but what really got me was that door slammed before me.

But all I did was shake my head. He said I should not do it again; he would buy us a TV set, one bigger than our neighbour's and a coloured one at that, as long as I promised not to smash windows again.

I nodded, Papa smiled, and we were friends again. Or so he thought.

My Grandmother's *Laing*

I only have to see taro (*laing*) leaves simmered in coconut milk for me to remember vividly my grandmother. She did not just save me from the longer spanking I would have received from my angry father, she also soothed me with stories of herself when she was young, of the imported apples and oranges that were abundant in the province of Masbate before the Second World War, when their town was a virtual gold mine. She also cooked the most delicious taro leaves swimming in coconut milk. I would watch her cook and I have committed to memory her recipe. Later, when I wandered far from home, in Scotland and parts beyond, I only had to cook taro leaves simmered in coconut milk, and I would be transported back to home, to my country of poverty and beauty.

Laing (Taro Leaves in Coconut Milk)

INGREDIENTS

500 grams of dried taro leaves
6 cloves of garlic, peeled
3 onions, chopped
1 thumb-sized ginger, peeled and chopped

½ cup cooking oil
250 grams of ground pork or ground chicken
A handful of shrimps or if too expensive, two tablespoons of shrimp
paste will do
1 ½ cups of coconut milk
Salt, to taste
Newly cracked pepper
Fish sauce (*patis*), to taste

In a mortar and pestle, she would pound the garlic, onions and
ginger. I would notice the flab on the underside of her arm flapping
like small wings when she pounded the spices. Then she would set
the spices aside. Next, she would heat the cooking oil in a pan, then
sauté the pounded garlic, onions and ginger. The shrimps and the
ground chicken or ground pork would follow. She would cook all
these for around five minutes until the shrimps had turned orange
and the ground chicken or ground pork had turned whiter. She
would add the coconut milk, and then season with salt, pepper,
and fish sauce. She would also add several pieces of *lada* (small red
pepper), if one was inclined to eat spicy food. Then she would let it
cook until the leaves were thoroughly done. My grandmother did
not touch the taro leaves. She just let them swim in the lovely lake
of coconut milk, since turning the leaves over and over would just
make them bitter.

Whether we talk about taro leaves or about life, it is sometimes
better to just let things be.

American Milk

My first day in school was wonderful. My mother had already taught me how to write, so I was not afraid any more of carrying my blue school bag with its lined pad paper, pencil and crayons. And because my mother also taught Grade Six in the building across the quadrangle, I knew she would always be nearby.

During the first month in school, the Americans from Clark Air Force Base in Angeles City came. The men were tall, with small, pink dots on their pale white skin. They came at 8 a.m. in a convoy of three vehicles. The first and last vehicles were six-by-six military trucks with uniformed men carrying long guns. In the middle was a white van with the men in white.

All the Grade One students formed two lines in the dry and treeless quadrangle. In front stood the two Americans, giving milk to all the children. The knots of children were excited, their voices buzzing, because we only saw Americans on TV. When my turn came, I looked up at one of the tall men, craning my neck until I thought it would snap.

The American smiled and laughed. 'Weather up here different, son. Have you had milk for breakfast today?'

I would have answered 'yes', along with dried fish and fried garlic rice, but he had already poured the milk in a tall, red plastic glass and gave it to me.

Like the rest of the children, I drank the milk in front of the Americans. 'They just wanted to be sure you will have enough energy for the school day,' Mrs Santos, my Grade One teacher, said later in class. She also wondered aloud what would have happened to us if the Americans did not come in 1898? 'Perhaps,' she said, 'we would still be all short, with flat noses and skin the colour of charcoal.' We sniggered because she herself was short, less than five feet tall, with nose as flat as her cheeks, and skin a few tones away from charcoal.

Since I had always been an obedient boy, I drank the milk in one go. It was thick and creamy and so unlike the Darigold evaporated milk that we drank at home, watered down by our housemaid, Ludy, so that the supply would last longer.

'Good boy,' the American said. 'You may keep the glass, but bring it again on Monday, for the next milk-drinking session.'

Later, we would return to our classrooms, which were Quonset huts that were remnants from the Second World War. In these hot and airless rooms shaped like small domes, we were fined one centavo for every 'native' word we used. We became spies of some sort, reporting to the English teacher our classmate who did not follow the English-only rule we had to follow the moment we set foot inside the school. That was nothing compared to the punishment for the wicked boys who constantly fought with each other: they were made to stay inside the small room at the back where the brooms were stored, facing the wall, and only came out after class was over.

In our English class, we mouthed 'things' by turning our tongues into a curve, with the 'h' aspirated so audibly. In this class, we also read hardbound books from America about John and

Annie and their dog Spot, who also seemed to speak in English. He barked 'arf-arf' and not 'bow-wow' the way the local Aspin, the dogs on the streets, did it.

So every week for the next ten months, the Americans in white came with their free milk, to make sure we would grow up as tall and healthy and cheerful as they were.

Ice Drop

Mama always bought my merienda or snacks. She did not want me to buy junk food and soda. Bad for the teeth, my mother with the whitest teeth would say.

When the bell rang for recess, I would always go to her classroom, Grade VI, Section 1. It was housed in a building hemmed in by star-apple trees, turning their leaves of translucent green in the sun. The leaves were green on top and brown below: their twin colours always amazed me.

I would cross the field, the wooden building looming into view. Then I would climb the concrete steps—one, two, three, four—and stop before the door just as Mama was about to dismiss her class. I would walk into the classroom just as her students were leaving. Some of the girls would pinch my cheeks; the boys would mess up my hair. I wondered why people bigger than me and twice my height would do that and I would just smirk.

I would go to Mama, her fingers and uniform smeared with chalk marks. That was how I always remembered her: wiping chalk marks that had somehow managed to whiten her sky-blue uniform. After this, she would hand me my snacks: boiled peanuts or coloured rice cakes topped with grated coconut, or fried plantains wrapped in sweetened rolls, everything except junk food. That, and orange juice in a tall blue Tupperware glass. Gratefully, I would wolf down the food, smile at her, then rush down the building, on to the wide field glittering with sunlight.

Since she prepared my snacks, she only gave me five centavos per day for my allowance. But in those days, five centavos could buy a large rectangle of *chicharon*, supposedly pork skin but just flour with artificial flavouring and that old reliable MSG.

Five centavos could also buy you a bar of Chocnut, crumbly chocolate with peanut bits that stuck to your gums, or a turn in the game of *bunot* in the school canteen. The game involved choosing a number, after which the storekeeper would peel away the layer of paper covering the number on the board. Whatever was attached to the number—a sheaf of Tex playing cards or five marbles, ten rubber bands or a plastic duck, a robot made of tin and painted red—would be your prize.

B ut one day I felt healthy enough from all of my mother's food, so when the canteen was transferred to the building farthest from Mama's classroom, I ate something she had forbidden me to eat: ice drop.

'It's so cold it will just give you tonsillitis again,' she would say, 'and then, you don't even know if it is clean.'

Nevertheless—

One day I saw the ambulant vendor in the school yard, standing under the dapple of acacia leaves. He was opening his Styrofoam ice box. I went to him. When I saw vapour rising from the mouth of the box, I took a peek.

Ice drop, indeed: shreds of young coconut, boiled red beans, milk and sugar forming a concoction frozen around a flat wooden stick. After looking to the left and then to the right, I bought one, walked as fast as I could, and only stopped when I was already out of everybody's view. I hid from my classmates because Mama had told them I always had tonsillitis when I ate something cold. More than once, someone had snitched on me and told my mother I had eaten a piece of ice drop.

A wall hid me from the world. I leaned against it and hungrily pulled away the paper wrapper. The ice drop had begun to melt, the sticky liquid trailing down my fingers. I licked my now-sweet fingers and then began nibbling at the ice drop.

First the top, full and swollen with shredded young coconut meat and red beans, letting the sweetness bloom in my mouth. Then the body (chilling my teeth, numbing my lips, but it didn't matter, it never did). I ate and ate and, in a few minutes, nothing was left but the stick. I went to the faucet to wash my hands, then returned to the boring Arithmetic class.

That night my tonsils began to itch. I wish I could stick my hand all the way down to the cavity of my throat to hold the thing that itched with my thumb and forefinger.

Then my mother began her ritual. She asked me if I took something cold, and I had no choice but to confess that I ate the ice drop. First, she scolded me for disobeying her, threatening to completely cut off my five-centavo allowance. Then she fixed me a glass of lukewarm calamansi juice (five small, round lemons squeezed into the water), with no sugar (yuccch!), and made me drink it.

Then she made me gargle a mixture of potent vinegar from fermented coconut sap and warm water. This was a 'cure' my father said he had learnt from his Thai classmate when both Asians were trying to survive their first American winter at the Air Force Academy in Colorado Springs.

Afterwards, my mother tucked me in bed, giving me a back rub. Like my grandmother, she would use Vicks Vaporub, her warm fingers kneading my back and chest. She would rub my neck and I would feel a calmness descend upon me. Only then would I drift into a sleep ripe with dreams.

The Piano

A month after they were married, Papa bought Mama a piano. It was an upright piano, its body darker than the colour of wine. Padre Pelagio was selling the piano because he had planned to buy a new Yamaha organ for the chapel.

Papa borrowed money from the Savings and Loan Association in the military airbase, added his savings from a year's stay in Colorado Springs as a military scholar, then one day brought Mama over to the chapel.

'But we have no choir practice today,' Mama protested loudly.

'I think Padre Pelagio wants to tell you something,' Papa answered.

Mama must have smirked (I inherited the same petulant smirk from her), put on her Catwoman sunglasses with its frame studded with rhinestones, threw a sheer red bandana over her permed hair, then sat beside Papa in our jeep.

Dust trailed the jeep. It was summer and the heat blew right into the very pores of your skin. The acacia leaves fell and the white houses snored in their siesta; the sun was an immense, intense eye in the sky. It blinked when Papa's jeep stopped before the chapel. Padre Pelagio, his belly round like a watermelon, waddled out of the rectory.

'Good afternoon, Father,' Mama said, kissing the hand of the priest.

'O *ano*, are you already here to get it?' the priest asked.

'Get what?' Mama asked.

Papa smiled smugly (the way all those smug Hollywood lead actors must have smiled), and then he led Mama inside the chapel.

'This,' Papa said, touching the ivory keys with the colour of moth wings, 'is my birthday gift to you.'

Seven years later, I would sit before this piano, required to practice three times a day by my teacher, who also happened to be my mother.

'But it's summer!' I wanted to protest. The dragonflies were hovering over the stream behind our house, their bodies the colour of amber and fire. Our home-made kites were waiting to be flown in the clear, blue sky. The fruit trees were waiting in the orchard— mangoes, guavas, *aratiles*, *duhat*—the fruits ripened by the sun, waiting for our young and greedy hands.

But I had to stay at home and play the piano! Sometimes, I would just sit in my room and sulk. But Papa would not let my sulking pass and he would make me sit before the piano. Then, he would instal himself on the perezosa and listen.

He would ask me to play *Sarung Banggi*, a love song from the Bicol Region where he and my mother were born.

Sarung banggi
sa higdaan
nakadangog ako
nin huni nin sarong gamgam.
Sa luba ko, katurugan,
bako kundi simong boses
iyo palan.

Dagos ako bangon
Si sakuyang mata iminuklat.
Kadtong kadikluman ako
ay nangalagkalag.
Kasu ihiling ko si sakuyang mata
sa itaas,
simong lawog nahiling ko
maliwanag.

Kadtong kadikloman
kan mahiling taka.
Namundo kong puso talos na nag-ugma.
Minsan di nahaloy idtong napagmasdan
sagkod nuarin pa man dai ko
malilingawan.

(One night
as I lay in bed
I suddenly heard
The singing of a bird.
I thought it was a dream
but it was your voice
that I heard.

I then rose at once
and opened my eyes wide.
In that darkness I looked around
and when I raised my eyes,
I saw your face very clearly.

In that darkness when I saw you,
My sad heart found happiness

at once.
Although I saw your image only briefly,
I will never forget
that night
forever.)

When I looked at my father, he was already asleep. Perhaps it was the heat. Or my bad playing. Or the song itself, carrying him on its wings, back to a past when he was still young, looking for the images of love on a night washed by the milky light of the moon.

The Man on the Moon

Like somebody with a PhD, Papa was explaining to my grandmother and me how the Apollo 11 would fly to the moon.

From blast-off at Cape Canaveral in Florida, the United States of America, to the rocket's head splitting from its tail to the actual landing on the moon—he explained all this with verve. First, he slipped his right arm in his brown imitation-leather slippers, tracing a trajectory. Then, slipper and hand separated, like moulting skin. Soon only one slipper was left, standing for the rocket landing on the cold, windless landscape of the moon.

That night we watched the Apollo 11 landing in our new coloured TV. A blur of images. *The Stars and Stripes.* Then the astronauts in their white, bloated uniforms, looking like aliens. The rocket blasting off, hurtling in space like a bright comet with a long tail, and then many hours later, there was finally the moon: full of craters deeper and wider than anything I had ever seen. After the Apollo 11 had landed on the moon, the three astronauts free-floating in space (*A small step for man, a giant leap for mankind*).

'The men on the moon,' my father said, 'the greatest country in the world staking its claim on a territory millions of miles away from home. One day, you will also study in that great country, my son.'

I would just look at him and eat more Chocnut.

Years later, my grandmother would bring me to Manila in one of her summer vacations. Nora Aunor—the short, brown actress whose rise to fame defied the colonial notions of beauty in the country, she whose eyes spoke a language of their own—had a new film called *Minsa'y Isang Gamu-gamo* (Once a Moth). The complete title: *Minsa'y Isang Gamu-gamo Ang Lumaban sa Lawin* (Once A Moth Fought A Hawk).

In the film, Nora plays a Filipina nurse named Corazon, whose ambition was to go to the United States and work there. She lived near Clark Air Force Base in Angeles City. One day, her younger brother was shot by an American soldier on the periphery of the base fence. During the preliminary investigation he was asked why and he said, 'I mistook the young boy for a wild pig.' Certified as doing official work the day the boy was shot, the American soldier was just flown back to the United States. No charges could be filed.

Another image: Corazon's grandfather (played by the magnificent Pedro Faustino) was already alive during the Philippine Revolution against Spain in 1896–1898, and later, the Filipino-American War from 1898–1904. As a young boy of ten, he wore *calzoncillos*, like long johns that reached down to the knees. Inside the sewn edges of his calzoncillos was a piece of paper folded many times over. It would contain, in code, the enemy positions, the number of the American soldiers, the tactics of the revolutionaries, whom the Americans called bandidos (bandits). When Corazon's grandfather saw the Americans landing on the moon, he asked, 'Oh, do they now own even the moon?'

That night, after a dinner of shrimps and sweet-potato leaves in tamarind soup, I went out to the backyard. Everything was silent as if the night itself was holding its breath. Beyond the acacia leaves, the moon rose clear across the Zambales mountains.

While helping her set the table, our housemaid Ludy had told me that there was a naked man on the moon even before the men of Apollo 11 came. She said he looked like the man in the five-centavo coin. So tonight, I took out the coin I had stolen from Papa's trousers and, in the light of the moon, I looked for the naked man in the coin. There he was: curly hair, a face well-chiselled, broad shoulders. His buttocks were firm and his legs, long and powerful. He was bending down, his body frozen in an arc. On his right hand he held a hammer, pounding something on the curved anvil in front of him. He was trying to make an object from ore, a shape from all that rawness. Like a god, he bent down patiently, hammering and hammering, waiting to be blasted by something like lightning, or a flash of revelation.

I squinted at the night sky, as if I had Superman's X-ray vision, or the eyes of Lee Majors, in *The Six Million Dollar Man*. But try as I might, beyond the huge acacia tree and the looming mountains, I saw no man on the moon. There was only a lighted disk suspended in the air many, many miles away, alone, beautiful and pure.

When the Wind Blew

Typhoon Yoling travelled at a dizzying 200 kilometres per hour. In its wake came a tail of fierce and terrible winds. Like the moon, it seemed to have raised water from the sea, for when it fell on the land, it rained so hard it seemed that the very skin of sky had been torn.

We had no classes for a week. It was cold and I woke up early. Rain fell like stones on the roof and the wind outside was moaning like a beast. We had breakfast of *champurrado* and fried fish. I ate two bowls of the sweet chocolate-flavoured rice porridge and five pieces of the fish. I returned to my bedroom and looked outside, at the day beginning to break. My fingers touched the windowpane. Cold, covered in mist. With my forefinger, I traced my initials. From my initials, I could see with sharp clarity the world outside my room.

Our duhat tree seemed to be getting a thrashing in the middle of the storm. Its small round fruits and leaves were whirling on their twigs, and the branches seemed to have gone mad, moving from here to there as if they were possessed by an evil spirit. They convulsed violently, and then came a sound that made my skin crawl. A low, loud moan, then a gust of wind that smashed at our duhat tree. Our tree tried to hold its ground, to weather the dervish wind, but I heard something snap. With my palm, I hurriedly brushed away the gathering mist on the windowpane. The tree had been split cleanly in two, around three feet from the base. The tree—fruits, leaves, and all—lay on the wet ground. I remembered the hot summers when I climbed this tree, its dark and sweetish fruits rubbed with salt and popped swiftly into the mouth, and I felt a pang run through me.

When my father turned on the TV set, there were widespread appeals for relief goods and aid. The whole of Central Luzon— those five provinces that were the country's rice bowl—was deep in floodwaters. An Air Force helicopter with media men inside took a pan of the area—water, water everywhere! When the choppers came closer, there were houses submerged in the flood, with only the angled, corrugated-tin roofs jutting out in the immense greyness. And on top of those roofs, like the inverted arks of Noah, huddled shadows. Not blackbirds flapping their wings. But as the helicopters came closer, the figures changed to people, their thin clothes sticking to rain-drenched skin. *Not waving, but drowning.*

And the reports flew thick and fast.

Of a woman whose whole family was completely wiped out ('I tried to save my children when the floods came rampaging at night, but their hands slipped from my grasp, and suddenly there was only water'). She was saved because she happened to be near the huge styrofoam box that contained the soda drinks they sold in their small variety store. When the floodwaters came, she grabbed the box, turned it upside down, and ran to the room where her children slept, to save them.

Of a town whose inhabitants were completely wiped out. Pabanlag (population: 5,000) was located between the mountains and an estuary that drained off to the sea. The mountains had been dutifully denuded of trees, thanks to the mayor who had found an ally in the provincial military commander and the corpulent governor who was so fat that he had begun to walk like a crab. There was gold in those hills, except they weren't the kind that could be beaten into the sheerest filigree, but acres of precious narra and mahogany trees that could be whittled down and shaped into tables and cabinets and chairs, especially now that there was a rage for 'modern antique', furniture newly carved but lacquered and painted to look like heirloom pieces.

So when the rains came, no century-old trees stood their ground to hold the water with their thick network of roots. Instead, the flood slipped down the mountains, like vomit. By that time, the river's estuary had been swelling and swelling. It had been raining for three days and the river had overflowed its banks. The town was now under three feet of water.

When the water rushed down the mountain, it cascaded like a great waterfall. The people said they heard the sound of a thousand hooves, louder and louder by the second, making the blood run cold. And then, complete darkness. The people were borne away by the swift and swirling water. In the dark, their fingers clawed, looking for something to hold: coconut trees, doors, windows, the very water.

When the darkness lifted, the whole town was gone.

Houses were wrenched away as if by the roots, and scattered miles and miles away from where they had originally stood. Broken windows, doors flung on the streets, blasted walls. And everywhere, the dead, pile upon pile upon pile of them. In the backyard of what was once his house, a man lay, his fingers in a half-curl, his open eyes staring blindly at the sun. On the street lay a mother embracing tightly her baby, wanting to shield her from the onrush of water in the darkness. And swept out into the sea, an old car with a whole family trapped inside. Around the car floated men and women with torn clothes and broken skin, their bodies bloated, floating and floating in the luminous blue of the sea.

Oh, after the flooding there were the usual recriminations against illegal logging. The president promised a thorough investigation that he said 'would not spare anyone. We will leave no stone unturned', he added in his ringing rhetoric broadcast in all TV and radio stations, 'to get to the bottom of this issue'.

The First Lady was the Head of the Task Force Yoling, which gave away relief goods like rice, sardine cans, salt, mung beans and soap stuffed into cotton bags with their design of faded flowers, recycled from B-Meg Poultry and Pig Feeds. The relief goods were stamped with 'GIFTS FROM THE FIRST LADY AND FAMILY', the words emblazoned in her favourite colour: fuchsia.

Old Woman on a Bridge
about to Crumble

In the aftermath of Typhoon Yoling, Papa and I did the marketing on Saturdays. Mama stayed at home during weekends, helping Ludy clean the house and the backyard from the detritus left by the typhoon.

My father brought me along with him because I know my mother's *suki*, her trusted and long-time vendor of fruit, vegetables, meat and rice. Into the labyrinth of the wet market my father and I went, each of us carrying a wicker basket. We stopped in front of Mrs Helen's stall spilling over with vivid reds and yellows and greens. The yellow flowers of the squash, like small and triumphant trumpets. The green leaves of the sweet potatoes, the leaves shaped like hearts. Young mountain ferns whose soft ends curled like commas. Lemongrass with roots hanging like an ancient beard.

Then we went to the fish section and looked for the young shark's meat that my father loved to simmer in coconut milk.

* * *

Kinunut (*Guinutay na pating* or shredded shark)

INGREDIENTS

1 kilo of *pating* or shark meat
½ cup coconut vinegar
Milk from 2 medium coconuts in 1 cup water
3 cloves garlic, crushed
1 medium onion, chopped coarsely
1 thumb ginger, shredded
1 teaspoon peppercorns, newly cracked
4 pieces finger pepper, cut to ¼-inch lengths
50 grams *kalunggay* (moringa leaves)
A pinch of salt to taste

Kinunut is the Bicolano word for 'shredded'. Here it refers to the method of preparing shark meat, this being the only recipe where the fish is shredded.

Shark meat is sold cut across in slabs.

Put the fish in a pot with enough water to cover it. Over high heat, bring the water to a boil. After five minutes, remove from the heat, then drain the water. This process removes most of the strong odour of the shark meat. With a knife, scrape off the scales of the shark (these have the look and consistency of rough sand) and then wash the meat. Shred the meat with a fork or a knife. Set aside.

In a wok over high heat, boil the coconut milk, garlic, onion, ginger and peppercorns. Stir constantly to prevent curdling. When the oil has oozed out of the coconut milk, add the fish and the vinegar. When the fish is almost done, add the finger peppers and then the moringa leaves. Do not stir because the leaves will turn bitter if you do so.

This dish is also favoured as finger food to be eaten with palm wine or ice-cold beer by the men in the provinces.

My father knows that last sentence only too well.

* * *

We finished in good time—under two hours—and I asked my father for my treat: some coins to buy my Chocnut. We also bought *Liwayway* magazine and Tagalog *komiks* for my grandmother. My father didn't want me to read the native fare, for he only encouraged me to read the *Manila Times* every day and the *Sunday Times Magazine*, which were all written in English. He had also subscribed to the *Reader's Digest,* whose tagline was 'America In Your Pocket'. I liked its vocabulary section, 'It Pays to Increase Your Word Power' by Peter Funk. I always used the new words I learnt in my theme papers in my class in English, to the great amusement of my teacher. Later, my father asked his brother, Conrado, who was working as a seafarer on a Norwegian oil tanker to send him a complete set of the *Encyclopedia Britannica*, whose hardbound volumes I patiently read, in the long and lonely summers of my childhood, the pages ranging from *Aardvark* to *Zygote*.

When my father and I got out of the market, the sky was already the colour of bruises.

'Oooppps,' Papa said, 'we better hurry up. The rain might fall again.'

So I climbed into the jeep and helped Papa arrange the two big wicker baskets of food on the back. And then the rain did fall, huge buckets of water pouring down on the earth. Papa drove slowly. Wind whipped all around us and Papa had to stop on the shoulder of the road so we could button down the plastic flaps on the side of the jeep to shield us from the rain.

Greyness was all around us. We could not see anything. Papa had turned the headlights on, and the lights tried to bore holes into the walls of the rain. We moved slowly, as if on a crawl.

When we reached the old wooden bridge, the river had risen and it was beginning to roar. In the dark we could not see the river but we could hear its deep, low growl. My hands began to sweat, and I wiped them on my shorts to dry them.

Suddenly, our headlights flashed on what looked like a dress flapping in the wind. A brown dress, and then the stooped back of an old woman in the shape of the letter C.

She was all alone in the rain.

'What does she think she's doing?' Papa said.

The woman did not seem to have seen us. She just stood there, on the wooden bridge that could crumble any minute now, looking far away, into the river and the rain.

Papa stepped out of the jeep and ran to her. His lips opened and shut. His thumb jerked back at our jeep, but the old woman did not even so much as look at him. Her hands just rested quietly on the concrete railing of the bridge.

Finally Papa gave up and ran back to the jeep. He backed up, swerved to the left, and then we moved away slowly, away from the old woman looking at the river swelling before her, her face impassive and fixed, just staring at a world that was beginning to end.

Sssssh

Ahhh, that sound, how can I forget that sound?

Dusk had fallen by then, and we were home. Papa always told us to be home as soon as the chickens had roosted on the star-apple trees in the yard. Ludy explained to us why, in her gentle Bicolano accent, her diphthongs rising and falling: 'You should be home before dark. Otherwise, *hala*, you would get in the way of the creatures who would be abroad as night falls.' Then she would enumerate all these creatures and their characteristics down to the last detail, as if they were her closest classmates in elementary school.

'The *kapre*,' she would say, 'is around when the moon is newly risen, the rain has just fallen, and an aroma is floating from the land. It is also around when the air begins to smell of a goat. The kapre looks like a human being, except that it stands more than ten feet tall. In fact, it is as tall as the acacia tree in our yard. Its eyes are as big as saucers and its lips are as thick as the branch of a tree. It is fond of smoking a cigar that never seems to grow short. You should see that red glow coming from the butt of its cigar, like an evil eye in the darkest night. The kapre scares people by shifting its form into a big dog, or a cat, a pig, or a water buffalo. When I was young, my father shot a kapre, but you know what? It just quickly turned into a slender bamboo stalk, flapping quietly in the wind. This giant does not like fire as well. It also avoids things made of gold and brass. My grandmother told me that if you ever catch a kapre and tie him to a tree, the next morning the giant would be gone, but there would be a pot of gold on the spot where the kapre had stood!'

From then on, I avoided the tall acacia tree in our backyard, whose generous shade shielded our small nipa hut from the sun. My father used the nipa hut as a storage area. When night fell, I also did not look outside at the acacia, whose leaves had curled up for the night, afraid that I would see the red, lighted end of a cigar ablaze in the night and then see the dark and hairy form of the kapre in our acacia tree.

After cooking *adobo*, chicken and pork marinated in soy sauce, vinegar, laurel leaves and garlic, its mouth-watering aroma permeating the kitchen, she would then tell me about the *manananggal.*

'This creature,' she would say as she ladled the food in the bowls, 'is like a dancer on a noontime TV show. It is very energetic. It could split not just its legs in mid-air or on the ground. Why, it could also split its body at the waist! By daytime, the manananggal assumes the form of a shy and demure woman, her eyes downcast when she walks on the street. But at night, oh my Lord, she becomes a beast with the most powerful wings. She leaves behind her lower body, which she hides behind the door. Then she heaves a deep sigh, like those young gymnasts whom we watched at the Olympic Games on TV, and then she would just fly. Her upper body detaches itself from the lower part and just merrily flies away. She then perches on the tops of roofs, looking for holes through which she could insert her long and vicious tongue. This tongue has an end that is as sharp as a razor. With a mere flick, it could slice open the belly of a sleeping person, and then the tongue would curl itself round the internal organs and suck the organs out. My grandmother taught me how to scare a manananggal, and I will also teach you how since you are a good boy. To scare a manananggal, you should throw a palm full of salt, three cups of vinegar, and three cups of chopped garlic out of the window while you are shouting out the names of these items. But do you know what is the fastest way to kill a manananggal? Why, you should thrust a spear right through its body. But if you want to be a manananggal yourself, then you should eat the food that had been touched by the manananggal's saliva. Or you should stay beside a manananggal as she slowly dies, because from her throat will issue a black chick. If you swallow that black chick, you will have the power of flight, which is actually what many people dream of doing. Imagine if you can fly?'

I shuddered at this thought. If my father was only nearby, he would tell Ludy to stop her silly stories and, instead, feed me my dinner and make sure I was doing my school assignments. But on many nights, he would wait for my mother to come home from elementary school before they would eat together. While waiting for her, he would read his Law books, for my father was also studying part-time at a law school 30 miles away from home. If not reading, then he would be talking to my grandmother in the living room, telling each other stories about my grandfather, a miner from Masbate who died at forty of a heart disease. My father knew that talking about my dead grandfather always cheered up my grandmother, who would listen with rapt attention, chewing on her betel nut and then spitting the red juice from her lips right through the open window, the juice falling right on the leaves of the ferns curled outside.

After feeding me and making sure my father was no longer there, Ludy would ask me if I still wanted to listen to just one more, just one more story before I studied my lessons or did my class assignments for the next day. Ludy was a good storyteller, with her eyes widening and her nostrils flaring, her voice getting louder and then sliding into a whisper, her fingers dancing in the very air, like Scheherazade, I thought, so that I told her, 'Yes, one more please, Ate Ludy.'

Her last story would be about the *mangkukulam*. 'My grandmother told me that the things reflected in a mangkukulam's eyes are always upside down. This may be why it does not look directly into another person's eyes. It usually assumes the form of an ugly woman who lives in a small nipa hut on the edge of the village. A truly marginal creature. But beware: the mangkukulam is powerful; it can hurt you so. It tortures its victims by entering their bodies, like dark air suddenly sinking into your skin, or placing a powerful curse on its victims. It can also prick a doll with pins, so that its victims will have headaches or stabbing pains all over the body, or even grow a tumour that no doctor could heal. Now, how do you fight a creature like this? Be prepared to have salt, vinegar, spices and artificial light. See? The spices I used to marinate our adobo are also potent against this creature! Moreover, the mangkukulam won't climb the stairs of a house with a pestle lying across the doorway. So now you know why I always put a pestle at the steps in the back of our house, so that no mangkukulam will climb here and get YOU!' She would say the last word with her eyes turning as big as the moon and her voice raised to a high pitch, her fingers like claws curled in my direction.

Off I would run to my room after this last tale. I would turn on all the lights, for I had been sufficiently scared by Ate Ludy's many stories. Then I would calm down and study my lessons for the next day. Or if there was no class the next day, or it was a weekend, I would then be allowed to watch TV.

My grandmother would be in her rocking chair and I would sit cross-legged in front of her, watching our modern-day gods.

The magical Shazzan with his head shaven, except for a ponytail sticking out from the top of his head. The caveman Mightor with the mighty club, which vibrates and emits waves of energy and light. The Japanese robot Gigantor, his body the size and shape of a big refrigerator, heaving himself from the earth to the air in an instant.

Once a week, the lights would suddenly go off as soon as darkness fell. And then the sound would come. When this happens, I would go to my grandmother and sit beside her, or hold her hand.

It was something we first felt rather than heard. A heavy gurgling in the air, like water swirling in the throat of a giant. Then it would come nearer and louder, what sounded like trucks lumbering blindly in the darkness. I never learnt what they were from either Papa or Mama. They never told me anything. From the gossip that Ludy had exchanged religiously with Nova, the housemaid next door, I heard they were the six-by-six military trucks again, transporting bodies in the night.

The day after the blackout, the chapel would be filled again. There would be stands of frangipani flowers and throngs of people. Sitting in front would be young women in black. Their young children wore strips of black ribbons on their chest. And lined in front of the altar would be the coffins, many coffins covered with the blue, red, and yellow of the Philippine flag.

'Who died?' I would ask Ludy in the middle of the Mass that we attended. Ludy sat beside me, while Mama conducted the choir. With every movement of her thin, wooden stick (I secretly called it her magic wand), the voices of the teenagers would rise and fall, become louder and softer, glide or float in the air. Papa would be with his friends, fellow military officers, standing near the heavy baroque door of the church, talking about their roosters and the cockpits, who was stealing from whom this time, clocking Padre Pelagio's sermon with their watches.

Ludy would answer my questions with a gesture. Forefinger on her lips. *Ssssh*, telling me both to shut up and to remind me never to ask questions without answers again, ever. Years later, whenever I saw a motel chain called the Queen Victoria, I would remember Ludy. Above the blazing neon sign is the figure of a young woman with big, wondering eyes, forefinger over her luscious lips. (*Sssssh*).

Wings of Desire

L ike me, my cousin Ramon was also the first-born of my Uncle Conrado and his wife, Emilia.

Papa woke me up early that summer. He told me to wash my face because we would go to Manila. My heart jumped with delight, especially when I saw that some of my clothes had already been stuffed in Papa's blue overnight bag.

Papa's eyes were sad. He kissed Mama goodbye, put my grandmother's hand on his forehead, and then we were gone. We took a pedicab to the gate. The young soldier on duty gave my father a crisp salute. Behind him stood the statue of a pilot cast in concrete, his eyes raised to the sky. Soon we were aboard a jeep bound for Guagua. As usual, the driver manoeuvred the jeep as if he were in the Indianapolis 500. His jeep zipped through the barrio road, the town's main road, and finally the highway at the same suicidal speed. Huts and wooden houses, buildings and plantations of sugar cane blurred before us. It always frightened me.

I closed my eyes and dredged my mind for prayers. Miss Honey Joy Tamayo of Catechism class said if you died with a Catholic prayer on your lips, you would go to heaven straightaway. So I began silently reciting the rosary, over and over again, the three mysteries repeated for the nth time from Floridablanca to Guagua, a distance of 20 kilometres, using my fingers to count the Our Fathers, Hail Marys and Glory Bes. If I did not go to heaven, I thought, at least I'd be good in Maths. The driver would suddenly step on the brakes, then rev the engine up again, swerve here and there, weaving in and out of our lane, the true king of the road.

Above him, a strip of mirror ablaze with decal stickers. *Basta driver, sweet lover. I only rest when I pee.* And directly in front of him, two women. On the left was the decal sticker of a vamp, her overripe body spilling out of her red bikini. The other was the veiled Blessed Virgin Mary, wearing layer upon layer of white clothes, a blue sash wound primly around her waist.

After 45 minutes, the jeep swung around the big plaza of Guagua. Then we got off and waited for the big bus bound for Manila. Usually they were air-conditioned Victory Liners, rare in those days, and once we had settled on our seats and paid for the tickets, Papa would begin to sleep, or rather, snore. I would be terribly embarrassed, but nobody seemed to mind, for almost everybody would fall asleep as the morning sun climbed higher in the clear sky of summer.

I would also try to close my eyes, but from behind my shut eyelids, I could see the tiny red spots formed by the sunlight. So I would open my eyes and then watch the world blur past me.

Three big covered carts pulled by a bull travelled slowly on the shoulder of the road. The carts contained wicker chairs and small tables, mirrors and hammocks, rattan baskets and shelves. The farmers from the north travelled all over Luzon after the harvest was over and the fields would lie fallow for months. They hoped to sell the things that they had woven and plaited. The carts were framed by a billboard advertising the many legendary bounties of the Philippines: the Banaue Rice Terraces carved into the mountains of Ifugao thousands of years ago; Mayon Volcano whose perfect symmetry no eruption could alter; the swift-sailing vintas of Zamboanga and the Santo Niño of Cebu City, luring the tourists to the sun, sea and sand of this calm and peaceful country.

The other billboards were from Filoil and B-meg Feeds, Ajinomoto Vetsin and Vitarich, as well as the Mobil gas station with the red flying horse. But the biggest billboard was the advert for YC Bikini brief, 'for the man who packs a wallop'.

I would check on my father, who, by this time, would be in deep sleep. Then I would look outside again, marvelling at the blue dome of the sky. It was rice-planting season again. Rice saplings had just been newly transplanted from their seedbeds, the slim, young leaves stirring in the wind. On the left rose Mount Arayat, a mountain shaped like a stump, smothered by white, fluffy clouds. The rice fields gave way to the brown nipa huts alive with the laughter of barefoot children with big bellies. Yellow rice grains left to dry on the sides of the road. White hens with red beaks cackling. People gathered around the transistor radio with its volume turned up so that everybody could hear other lives endlessly twisting and turning from the morning melodrama. The new wood-and-cement houses built for their parents by young men and women working in the Middle East. The abandoned mansions of the sugar barons, their dry fountains and wide gardens now choked by weeds, the heavy wooden doors now shut. And then the baroque churches, covered with moss and lichen, cratered by wind and rain. And in the air, the heavy, cloying smell of molasses from the mills of Pampanga Sugar Development Company or PASUDECO, inducing me finally to sleep. Later, this sugar mill would become a mall, like many of the buildings in the archipelago, grey and air-conditioned boxes filled with colourful things, but today, it was still a sugar mill whose sweet, sweet smell was filling me with such lethargy.

* * *

Manila burst like a bucket of icy water thrown on the face. The Andres Bonifacio Monument loomed (the proletarian hero frozen in a voiceless scream), the bus deftly circling the roundabout, and down we went to EDSA, the unbearable smell of the Cloverleaf Market, the diesel fumes darkening the air. We got off in a Cubao that still had no shopping malls, just small speciality shops and a row of big cinema houses. Then the jeep ride to Santa Mesa, so very fast with the miniature steel horses on the hood seemingly clop-clopping in the wind, the thin plastic strips of many colours flying, the jeep swerving, going up and down a bridge. Then here we were.

My uncle lived in his in-law's house on a strip of government land behind the motels of Old Santa Mesa. *Seven Seas, Heaven Sent, Erotica, Exotica* – I still recall their names in a breathless rush, these places where supposedly illicit love happened between people not married to each other, as my grandmother would say. Down we went, down, down the rough steps hewn out of stone. The wooden houses seemed to breathe into each other. One's kitchen ended where another's bedroom began. The alleys coiled round and round like intestines. And when the rainy season came, everything turned muddy and a perpetually green slime covered the ground for days.

After Papa and I had turned this way and that, poking into someone else's living room and scanning another's open bedroom, we reached the place—a one-storey affair at the foot of the stairs of an old wooden house.

Even at noon, bright lights burnt in the living room. The candelabra's fingers glowed. Under the lights, the coffin of my cousin Ramon.

My Aunt Emilia broke down at the sight of Papa. '*Manoy*, Mon is gone,' she wailed. 'What will I do?' Sobs tore from her chest, and the old women around her also began to cry like a chorus. They were all in black. Like a flock of crows. Papa let her go on.

She babbled that if she only knew Ramon would sustain a bad fall from a basketball game and bash his head, her son who was torn away from her by the doctor's forceps . . .

'I shouldn't have allowed him to play in that game. *Manoy*, should I tell Conrado?'

Silence. Papa seemed to weigh his words very carefully. Then, looking straight into my aunt's eyes, actually looking through her, he said: 'I think it would be best not to tell Conrado. I know my brother very well. He'll take it badly. He might . . .' Papa sighed deeply. He suddenly looked tired and very old. 'He might even jump from the ship if he hears about it.'

My aunt sank silently on the sofa. She cried wordlessly. It was painful to look at her. I stood up and walked over to the coffin of Ramon.

Atop the glass was his photograph taken a month ago, so very young, his eyes like clearest water. In his photograph, the gold First Honour medal shone on his white polo shirt. Leis of white jasmine buds and yellow-green *ylang-ylang* flowers were hung around the photograph. And then, I looked down at him.

In my dream, my Uncle Conrado has come home. He has left behind him the North Sea cold enough to break your bones. Now he is borne by waves that have slowly shaped themselves into the whitest of wings. The world below is a blue nothingness. The bird glides slowly, reaching an archipelago of the bluest sea and the greenest islands, until it reaches the brown filth that is Manila. The bird alights finally at Old Santa Mesa, and my uncle slides down its feathery body. He waves farewell to the strange, magnificent bird, which nods its head in acknowledgement. And then just as suddenly, the bird is gone.

Down, down, down the steps hewn from stone. The air closing in around my uncle, darkness descending, a door opening and closing on its one rusty hinge. *Ramon? Ramon? Where is my son Ramon?* Words from the palest lips. The electric volt of pain crackling from one nerve ending to another.

Sometimes, when we call out a name, even the very wind crumbles.

How Good That Friday Was

When the temperature began to rise so high that it threatened to make the thermometer explode, trust that Holy Week was here. I turned eleven years old that Holy Week. My birthday fell either before, during, or after the Holy Week when Jesus Christ suffered, died and rose again during the resurrection. When I turned eleven, I suddenly had a spurt of growth, reaching a height of five feet and four inches, my arms and limbs as long and as thin as bamboo stalks. But my head remained the same. It was as big as a watermelon, my eyes like the black seeds of this rotund fruit.

That morning, my mother gave me a *palaspas*, the young leaves of coconut folded and woven to form small globes and arcs, even fingers tapering to the sky. The *palaspas* would always be yellow green, the colour of the *ylang-ylang* flowers that perfumed our backyard.

We all went to the Mass. The churchgoers were more hushed than usual, striking dutiful poses of piety. A woman was worrying her rosary beads behind me, her eyes tightly closed. Her eyelashes seemed to flutter, like the wings of a butterfly coming out of the cocoon, and I controlled the impulse to touch her trembling eyelashes. My sexy classmate Mariani was standing on the next pew, her fingers forming a steeple. Any moment, I thought Mariani would raise her hands, spread them apart and shout 'DARNA!', turning her lacy white dress into Darna's red silk bikini, the Supergirl about to fly in the vast blue sky.

The long sermon of the now white-haired and semi-senile Padre Pelagio made the men look at their watches, to check if their timepieces were dead again. One or two even took off their watches, put them to their ears, and then shook them with vigour. The other men slowly walked out of the chapel, out on to the big garden with its bright bursts of *santan* flowers, to smoke. When the Mass was finally over, Padre Pelagio descended from his pulpit, holding a bowl full of holy water. He dipped the stick that picked up the holy water, then sprinkled the water all over the *palaspas* we had earlier raised for him. Droplets of the holy water would fall on us, 'like manna from Heaven', I remembered my Cathechism teacher saying, morsels of white and edible substance falling from the sky to feed the Israelites during their travels in the inhospitable desert for forty years following the Exodus.

Suddenly the colour of the air turned lemony green, humming.

Tuesday, Wednesday, Thursday . . . the countdown began. My grandmother forbade us from taking a bath until Jesus Christ had come back to life. In the coma-inducing heat of summer—sometimes the temperature blasted past 100 degrees Fahrenheit—not taking a bath would be an act enough to pay for all your sins mortal, venial and in-between; done in the past, present, and future; whether committed in your walking life or on the slippery landscapes of your dreams.

We usually stayed home on Good Friday, listening to the Seven Last Words on the transistor radio with circuitous and flowery explanations from the politicians, their voices grainy with sorrow. Or we would go to the chapel. While there, I would pretend to listen as the seven generals of the military airbase explained to us Jesus Christ's Seven Last Words before He was hung on the cross.

They would all be there:

1.   The general who had a mistress in every town within a radius
     of 50 kilometres from the military airbase.
2.   The general who headed finance and logistics and, of course,
     would line his pockets first than buy new combat boots for the
     military men murdering the Muslims in Mindanao.
3.   The general who wore all the medals (spurious or not) he had
     won, gleaming like bottle caps on his chest.
4.   The general who had cornered the forest concession for the
     still-virginal forest on the edge of town, on the slopes of the
     Zambales mountain ranges. He headed the environmental
     programme of the base.
5.   The general who was so turned on by the smell of gunpowder
     that he led military operations in the south that not only
     decimated Muslim men, but also women, old people, and
     children; bud, flower and fruit. His mission was to banish
     the brave and freedom-loving Muslims on whose sharp, fatal
     kris—double-edged, serrated swords that could decapitate
     cleanly and swiftly—the sun glinted.
7.   The general who said he did not intend to die. Thus, the main
     road was named after him, the park after his wife, and the three
     commissary buildings after each of his sons.

But enough of this game of the generals!

And so one Holy Week, we spent Good Friday in San Fernando,
the capital city of the province. My father was driving our
jeep. My mother sat beside him, determined to be poised even if
the wind blasting from the window was strong enough to crumple
her red bandana. I sat at the back, eating *lanzones* from a plastic
bag, peeling and popping into my mouth the fruit the colour

of pearl, careful not to bite into the seed which had the most bitter taste.

I looked outside—sugar-cane fields stretching into infinity, nipa huts and wooden houses roasting in the sun, a warm hush falling over everything. It is Good Friday, after all, when the whole archipelago was burdened with the death of the Saviour and the Redeemer. I went with my parents because there was nothing else to do. If only I had a brother or sister, I could at least play Scrabble with them, or climb trees when our parents had gone away. And incorrigible kibitzer that I was, I also wanted to see Daniel Rexroth, Jr have himself nailed on the cross.

As my father put it, Daniel had a yearly vow to have himself nailed until his American G.I. father, who had returned to the United States just before Daniel was born, would return to the P.I., the Philippine Islands of old. And like the great General Douglas MacArthur, the father would return and spring Daniel from the nails of poverty with an American visa, preferably immigrant, and then on to the Kingdom of Citizenhood. Daniel said in media interviews that his persistence would trump the naysayers; he would reach his dreams.

The nailing to the cross was held in the middle of the barren rice fields in Barangay Pedro Cutud, San Fernando, in the insane heat of summer. Gathered around Daniel were similarly shirtless men, their faces covered with white cloth. Earlier, they had asked other people to use broken glass to make small wounds on their backs. Then, they deepened the wounds by flagellating their backs with a whip made of rope tipped with split bamboo. Glittering shards of glass were also glued to the ropes. The *whoosh* of the whiplashes biting against the skin, the flagellants' backs turning into a merthiolate colour, the blood even splattering on the shirts and faces of the passers-by.

And then there was Daniel. He winced as the nails were driven into the palms of his hands. Rivulets of blood dripped down his hands and he looked at the sky with agony in his eyes. The Americans recorded everything with their video cameras; the reporters spoke into their microphones. But I walked away from the rice field toward our jeep, telling myself that when I grow older, I would spend my Holy Week in the mountain town of Sagada and watch the fog erase everything, hut, hill and mountain, or walk on the calm beaches of Palawan, as the sun drowned.

Of Cakes and Palaces

After Holy Week, my Papa's second cousin visited us. Auntie Millet had taken the train from Albay to Manila, then hopped on the bus from Manila to Pampanga, the moment she heard the news.

Her son, Berto, had joined her other son, Noel, in Manila. The older Noel worked for a construction company owned by one of the president's cronies. One of the company's biggest projects was the Manila Film Centre. Billed as Asia's answer to the Parthenon, this magnificent cinema house would be built on the soft, reclaimed land on Manila Bay.

'There is a hole in the universe,' the First Lady said on national TV last week, zapping the *Voltes V* cartoon which I was then watching, to my great annoyance. Later, the president would even ban the *Voltes V* cartoon for being 'too violent'. But on this day, all the TV stations dutifully covered the First Lady's interview with the Foreign Correspondents' Association of the Philippines. She was wearing her long, powder-blue national dress with its sleeves like butterfly wings. The diamonds on her ring turned into petals of fire when she spoke. She continued: 'From this black hole comes the energy field of the universe. This energy field, my friends, is directed at my beloved country, the Pearl of the Orient Seas.

Thus, we are truly blessed, because this positive force will lead us to progress, to our dream of development for our dearest Philippines.'

The foreign correspondents were unusually quiet. The grave air was broken by a question from a Filipina who was as tall and graceful as a bamboo. She asked: 'Ma'am, do you intend to write a book about it?' Her name was Dada Walana, a poet who became a journalist who became an official spokesperson of the press bureau.

'Now, that's a good idea,' the First Lady said spontaneously. 'That would be a worthy follow-up to my first book of speeches, which became a bestseller.'

And so the brothers Relova worked at the construction site of the Manila Film Palace by the bay. The newspapers would report that the First Lady, who was suffering from her incurable insomnia, would sometimes leave the palace in her long, black stretch limousine, the sirens from her escort cars wailing in the night, and visit the bay. Her long, black hair would be lacquered and erect even at three o' clock in the morning. Her red silk scarf would billow in the cold wind coming from the dark sea and she spoke to the foreman with such urgency.

The captive media trumpeted everything the First Lady said, to wit: 'This building has to be finished in 77 days. Remember, seven is the president's favourite number.' Then she smiled, but not too widely, for she had just gone through her seventh face-lift.

At least, the clandestine opposition press said, this project was a far cry from her last one. As minister of human habitation, she had ordered the building of a low-cost housing project on top of the bald Antipolo Mountains. Not a bad idea, really, except that she only built 5,000 white American Standard toilets.

And like a game of ping-pong, the administration and the opposition press reported on the same event, but from different angles. They could very well have been talking about two parallel universes.

'Cleanliness is next to Godliness,' the First Lady intoned during the ribbon-cutting ceremony, which was front-page news for the crony press. 'Our many dispossessed know that, and so they will build their own houses *around* these toilets. We gave them something they can build on.' And so the 5,000 white toilets gleamed in the afternoon sun for many months.

The opposition press said that the Antipolo Mountain, baking in the heat and studded with white toilet bowls, came to be known as Kubeta Village, or Toilet Village. Pretty soon, the toilets all magically vanished, cannibalized by the dispossessed.

This, though, promised to be different, this Film Centre by the gleaming bay.

Auntie Millet was now here, standing silently outside our white door. Her clothes were the colour of ash. Red veins ran across her eyes. She had just travelled for 10 hours in an old rickety train rattling on the tracks. Her son Noel had returned to the building site, to continue digging.

Mama sat beside Auntie Millet and listened, her eyes beginning to tear as Noel's mother spoke. I pretended I was merely watching *Student Canteen* on TV, but I listened intently to her story. In the end, she did not cry. She just sat wordlessly in our living room, an old woman with something so deep in her eyes you could not touch it.

Her son Noel told her that the pressure was strong for the workers to finish the construction of the Manila Film Centre. So they just kept on mixing sand and stone, water and cement, pouring them into shaky foundations. They cobbled together one storey after another, the whole structure looking like a honeycomb. And one fine, windless day, the bamboo scaffolding just collapsed, sending the men falling down into a pit of quick-drying cement.

Noel was outside, shovelling sand into a small lake of cement, stone, and water when he heard the screams. He ran inside because his brother Berto was there. The workers had gathered around the pit of cement beginning to dry. Beneath this lay the other workers, including Berto.

Quickly, the workers grabbed their shovels and pickaxes; they even used their very hands to rescue their fellow workers trapped under the rubble. Bits of cement flew and hit Noel in the eyes. He closed his eyes for they had begun to water – the grains scratching against his eyeballs – but he kept on hitting the cement with his pick axe, faster and faster, as dusk began to fall and the bay outside started to display Manila's magnificent sunset.

But the next morning they were still trying to crack the cement. Dark circles had begun to ring their eyes. Their stubbles were shadows. They had begun using electric drills. The sound of so many drills was enough to make one deaf for life. But the men kept on drilling. From time to time, they would hit something solid under the cement. Noel was drilling with the purest concentration, his eyes focused on the point where the layer of cement splintered into bits, when a jet of blood suddenly struck him.

First on the knees, arcing across his thighs, and then splattering on his chest. It was then that he began to cry. He dropped his drill and his hard hat and ran, ran home to the squalor of the slums in Malibay where he lived, grabbed an old duffel bag, threw some clothes into it, and took the first bus back to Albay.

No one seemed to move while Auntie Millet told her story. She spoke quietly, softly, to her second cousin, my father, in tones that were respectful, even somewhat distant.

Instantly, Papa went to his boss, the military general, who called up the other military generals in Manila, who then called up the contractor, etcetera. After a whole day spent making these calls, being shunted from one general's office to another, they finally managed to get through to the press bureau.

But Dada Walana—bright and cheery as a parakeet—informed Papa that, 'Yes, Sir, there was, indeed, a *minor* incident at the Manila Film Centre, but only *two* workers were slightly injured. They were promptly given medical attention upon the First Lady's express instructions, who went there as soon as she heard of the news.'

A week later, Noel would come to us to fetch his mother and bring her home back to Albay. He looked like a ghost. He had lost half his weight, his shoulders stooped from a week of non-stop digging. In broken words, he said the authorities had wanted the construction of the Manila Film Centre to go on as scheduled. And so the foreman had ordered the guards to keep Noel and the other relatives out of the construction site as buckets of fresh cement were poured on the site, stopping the river of blood from welling up from below.

Then they resumed building the Film Centre.

That would, however, come later, for on this day, after helping Ludy cook *Tagalog* beef steak marinated in soy sauce and small lemons and taro leaves simmered in coconut milk, the mother of Berto and Noel walked to our backyard, past the star-apple trees, stopped under the acacia, and just looked clear across the dry rice field at the wall in the distance – the thick, grey wall separating our military airbase from the rest of the world.

A Dreadful Saturday Afternoon

It was a dreadful Sunday afternoon, the kind when it would be impossible to sleep in my room. The sun itself seemed to have taken refuge inside our house, its rays of heat buried inside my skin.

I would run into the backyard, looking at the play of shadow and light on the serrated leaves of the aratiles tree. Then I would climb the tree heavy with its globes of small, red fruits. From the highest branch, I would pretend as if I were jumping from the edge of a cliff. The ravine would be our roof, a makeshift bed carpeted with soft, green leaves.

From that height, nothing seemed to move me.

And from that height I eavesdropped on the chatter of adults without being caught. So that summer, while busy eating aratiles fruits on the rooftop, who would cool themselves on the shadow cast by the tree but my two aunties? That day, my mother's spinster sisters, *Tita* Bella and *Tita* Armida, were having a snack of glutinous rice cakes topped with grated coconut meat and cold glasses of soda.

They raised their heads and looked around discreetly, with only their eyes moving. When they noticed that nobody was around, the two sisters began their stories.

'The Our Lady of Peace and Good Voyage in Antipolo Church is more powerful than the Our Lady of Perpetual Help that is venerated in the Baclaran Church,' Tita Armida began.

'That may be true,' answered Tita Bella, 'but tell me, how could you hear Mass in Baclaran when around you would be the squealing of pigs being butchered for the lechon?'

Tita Armida, who loved to spin a tale, answered: 'Bella, have you heard the story of the two young lovers in Baclaran?'

'No.'

'Well, well then, listen. A pair of teenagers would hear the Holy Mass at the Baclaran Church on a Sunday afternoon just like this. But really, they would just go to a motel from across the church and do it there, while all along, the pigs squealed and the Dutch priest intoned the *Sursum Corda* in an accent that nobody could understand. These young people, Mother of God, are such animals.'

'They are, Armida. They are,' cooed Tita Bella.

'Anyway, these teenagers have been telling this lie for two consecutive Sunday afternoons, but on the third Sunday, something happened.'

'What?' Tita Bella asked. Her fork must have been frozen in mid-air, between the white saucer and her big mouth.

'On the third Sunday afternoon, in the fever of their lovemaking, her vaginal muscles just suddenly locked. *Locked*. He could not withdraw much as he wanted to, because she was squeezing him so tightly. Then the pigs squealed for their lives and the Dutch priest raised his golden ciborium and the two young lovers, oh God did not bless them, good for them, they were beginning to turn very pale indeed.'

'And then?' was all Tita Bella could mutter.

'And then, she began to scream and scream and scream. The room boy wondered why she was screaming her lungs out, for the couple had been there twice before. But when the room boy heard *him* scream, the kind of scream that would make the blood run cold, he knew that something was wrong. So the room boy grabbed the key attached to a stainless-steel key ring and ran to the room of Mr and Mrs Angeles (the names they wrote in the guest book with its synthetic-plastic cover), and found the couple joined, indeed, to each other. The room boy gasped, ran down the rickety wooden stairs, and fetched the doctor who lived down the block.'

'Praise be to God,' was all Tita Bella could say.

'Well, it turned out that the doctor was a devoted Catholic who was scandalized the moment he pushed the white door of the motel room and came upon the two lovers joined to each other. After raining down a mountain of curses on the couple in dishabille, he took out his syringe and injected a muscle relaxant on her. And then the doctor continued to give them the sermon of their lives, *JesusMaryJoseph*, doing this in the middle of a Sunday afternoon, right in front of the Baclaran Church! The young couple was almost dying from shame because the medicine was taking a long time to take effect and their organs were very sore. Already.

'And then?'

'But when the medicine did take effect, he quickly withdrew and put on his clothes as fast as he could. She also covered herself modestly with the white, cotton blanket, grabbed her crumpled clothes, said "Thank you" to the doctor in a sweet voice, and then walked to the bathroom. When she came out, she was wearing a white dress cut way past down the knees with a blue sash wound around her slim waist. The doctor told them that the wisest thing would be to go to Baclaran Church that afternoon, confess their sins, and attend the Holy Mass.'

'Indeed. They already missed two Masses—and on such a pretext! I shudder at the thought of what would happen to their souls.'

'You are so very right, Bella. And so, ushered by the doctor on one side and by the room boy on the other, seemingly ushered by an old angel and a young acolyte, the teenaged couple finally went to the Holy Mass that they, uh, missed for the last two Sundays.'

After hearing the conclusion of this tale between my two spinster aunties, I bit into the smooth, red skin of my aratiles. Its small, white and moist seeds lay scattered on my palm.

How I Spent My Summer Vacation

Her arrival was signalled by the heat that seemed to quiver in the air. After my two mad aunties had left the house, it was my cousin Naomi who stayed with us during that unforgettable summer. For the first time I had a companion I could talk to, aside from Luis.

My cousin Naomi was bright and sassy. My auntie had died just after she had given birth to Naomi. My uncle-in-law never got over my auntie's death. He sank into drunkenness and despair so deep he would often blame the young Naomi for her mother's death. So since then, she had been shunted off from one relative to another. I really did not know how she survived with hardly any scars at all, for my relatives had varying degrees of madness.

That summer we took to each other, like two long-lost friends. Every afternoon, Naomi and I fed my father's menagerie. First, we would feed the pigs. We would mix the leftover food with the rice bran and water. Then we would pour the soggy mixture on to the wooden troughs made by my father. Upon smelling their food, Miss Piggy and her current lover, whom we called Kermit, would grunt the grunt of the truly hungry—their snouts sniffing the air—and would then rush over to the trough. You could feel how delighted they were when they began to eat.

Next, we would feed the chickens. We would dig our fingers into the warm lake of dry rice seeds stored in the tall tin can of biscuits. The seeds would be mixed with the poultry feed, which we would sprinkle on the narrow bamboo trough tied to the chickens' cages.

Finally, it was time to feed the ducks. We would mix everything—leftover food, rice seeds and poultry feed—and pour the mixture on the deflated car tyres split in halves and set on the ground. Soon the ducks would waddle in, then dip their red and orange beaks on to the slop.

The ducks excited me most, for they were not hemmed in by bamboo cages or by a pen. After having their fill, they would wander about the backyard for a walk to let their food settle. The ducklings would then follow their mother duck, like the Pied Piper of Hamelin, down the slope, toward the clear stream running on the edge of our yard.

That summer, however, half of the duck eggs had not yet been hatched. 'They must hatch soon,' I told Naomi one afternoon while we were playing Scrabble. 'In a few weeks, the rains would fall and the eggs would start to rot.'

Naomi always beat me in Scrabble, which was a feat because nobody in the neighbourhood could. She looked up from the letters on the plastic green tiles that she had arranged on the wooden block before her. Her eyes flashed wickedly under her bangs.

'Okay, come on,' she said, then hoisting her right foot over the wooden bench. I followed her quick, tomboyish gait out of the back door, then on to a hot afternoon in a world beginning to shrivel.

We walked on and on—past the faucet where Ludy did the laundry, the wall where I sometimes pissed when my father was in the toilet and I could no longer hold it, the sweet potatoes with their leaves coloured purple and green, the taro and the tomatoes and the eggplants, toward a rusty roof as tall as me.

Beneath the roof was a wicker basket full of dried banana leaves. And in the middle of the nest lay the five unhatched duck eggs. Naomi smiled to herself, then quickly licked the underside of her lips. It was a gesture that I had already learnt to read. In Scrabble, it meant she would put on the board a set of letters, carefully now, whose total score would be a double, even a triple! In school, it meant striding on to the stage at year's end, to claim again the gold medal for First Honours, pinned on her blouse by whoever amongst our relatives was adopting her for the moment. In the afterglow of sunset, our proud relative would beam before the crowd, showing them that, indeed, Naomi and himself or herself had come from the same gene pool.

Now, Naomi and I sat on our haunches. She was holding an egg in her hand—a whole world cupped by her fingers. She touched the top of the egg, then slowly, slowly, she began to peel it. Her fingernail was as smooth and as polished as the egg she was holding. Intently, I looked at her fingers, holding my breath as the shell cracked. A tiny yellow head would emerge from the shell, its feathers soft-looking and moist. Suddenly the eyes opened—eyes bright and wet—and Naomi would smile. I would say something cheerful and stupid, as was my wont then and now. Naomi would not answer but would continue peeling away the rest of the shell until the whole duckling was free. Then, she would set the duckling on the ground. It would look up to us, to Naomi and I, and then it would flap its tiny wings merrily.

With her pulse moving in her temples, Naomi wordlessly peeled away the shells of the four other eggs. All of the ducklings were alive, and only when she had freed the fifth duckling did Naomi let out a whoop and jump, her loud laughter waking the very air.

By then the duck's mother had come, Lazy Mama, Naomi would tease it, come to fetch her newly hatched brood. The five ducklings were flexing their young wings, turning their small heads this way and that, while a faint wind stirred their soft, yellow feathers. Upon seeing somebody who looked like them – only much bigger – the ducklings would form a queue and follow their mother, five small spots of sun. And then they were gone, their wings waving at Naomi as they waddled clumsily after their mother, who would go down the stream to welcome her ducklings to the world, with a grand baptism by water.

Later two of the ducklings would die, carried away by the raging floods that came in the wake of the year's first typhoon. And was she seventeen then, (or eighteen?), when Naomi ran away from home with a classmate from her university.

'*Ingrata*!' my relatives fumed. 'How ungrateful!' Then they would add, 'How stupid, too! What's a good head for if she didn't use it? She should've finished her studies first before falling for this *tentacion*, the temptation offered by the city. The man himself was working his way through school, how would they then survive? Could love feed them every day of their lives? Could you go to the grocery and pay for a can of milk with love?'

But Naomi did return home, after the man had left her. She did face the lash of words from my Tita Bella and Tita Armida and other concerned relatives, a firestorm that would have made the perennial villain of Philippine cinema, Zeny Zabala, look like a nun. Naomi bore everything in stoic silence. Her belly became bigger. And she sank deeper and deeper in the swamp of her sadness.

A week after giving birth to a boy, she just died.

'Cancer of the cervix,' an uncle who was visiting us, said, blowing on his hot cup of *chocolate eh*. 'That's the problem with young people nowadays, they don't listen to us older folk any more. See? She got that sickness because she had been *tampered with* at an early age. God doesn't approve of such things.'

He would make the *tsk tsk tsk* sound, like that of a lizard at sundown, then drink his cup of thick chocolate, my uncle who read the Good News gospel during the Mass back in the province. I hope it scalds you, I thought as I looked icily at him. I hope the hot chocolate would burn you, pour out of your mouth, your nose, your ears, the other orifices of your holy body.

Plaza del Fuego

M y father, mother, grandmother, Ludy and I were watching the Nacionalista Party's political meeting on our TV screen.

This was the grand—and final—meeting before Election Day for the country's new senators and congressmen. The NP had chosen to hold theirs at Plaza del Fuego, the square beside Quiapo Church, its blind statues looking down at the hawkers vending everything, from something green and swimming in a bottle of Tanduay Rhum, supposedly a potion for delayed menstrual flow (read: an abortifacient), to an old woman perpetually saying the rosary, her fingers moving on the black plastic beads, selling her prayers for your dearly departed.

Plaza Miranda was small, indeed, bordered on the north by a stand of decrepit stores; on the west by the Mercury Drug store, its tall white facade always backlit by hundreds of fluorescent lamps; on the south by España Avenue, choking with jeeps and their diesel fumes. An air pollution indicator was once installed on the fringe of the plaza, to dramatize the First Lady's concern about the inhabitants of her new domain, the City of Man newly carved from the three cities and thirteen municipalities around Manila. But barely a year after this project, the index had stopped working. Its pollution indicator had been fixed at HIGH, the button's light burning red, like the angry eye of a beast. In a stroke of fine irony, the diesel fumes themselves, the toxic chemicals roiling in the air, had turned the Index into rust.

And so, we had on prime time TV the senatorial line-up of the Nacionalista Party, a mélange of lawyers, academicians, libertarians and landlords. No movie stars yet, no sports heroes yet, no comedians yet—that would come later, when the country had completely gone to the dogs.

Speech after speech, words rising and falling, embroidery and fluff. While watching the proceedings on TV, I was already beginning to fall asleep on my grandmother's warm lap. And suddenly, a sound like quick thunder came from the TV screen. I started and sat bolt upright in my seat. On the screen, people were running; smoke was beginning to foul the air, and then there was complete darkness.

My father stood up and turned the AM radio on, with its shrill, surreal announcers.

There was a time when Domingo Langit was covering a student demonstration. In this country of very excitable radio commentators, he spoke the slowest. He asked one of the young boys what he thought of General V. The boy snapped: 'Well, he's a Goebbels.'

Forthwith Domingo Langit said, with the whole archipelago tuning in, 'I have a dictionary with me here, inside station ABC-XYZ's mobile van, but I cannot find ge-bells. Please give me a second, folks, I'll just look up the meaning of the word.'

But tonight, in the wake of the explosion, Domingo Langit was in full fettle, in his finest form. 'I have a breaking news. A bomb had just exploded in Plaza del Fuego,' he said, his voice looping faster than the usual slow spiral. 'Many people are hurt. Senator Jovito Salonga seems to be in bad shape. One of the senator's wives had her left foot in a horrible twist. With her fan she is waving for help. Blood, oh Lord Jesus Christ, blood is everywhere.'

The body count came the morning after (five killed, 120 wounded, half of them in serious condition). One of those who died was the brilliant photographer Max Vicoy. The papers splashed the photo of this tall, thin man, his clothes soaked in blood, holding on tightly to his camera before he finally died.

Grains of Memory

I was already an avid reader of the *Philippines Free Press Magazine* even when I was just eleven years old. My father would buy this magazine from the commissary every week. I read the poems and the feature articles, the essays and the stories, even if I could not understand all of them. However, things would remain with me, like grains of sugar that have settled at the bottom of a cup.

One day in January, the president delivered his State of the Nation address. We were watching him on TV. Sometimes, the camera would pan the crowd of student activists outside, then back to the majestic halls again, with its high, white ceiling and smooth, marble posts. This was where the president delivered his State of the Nation address.

'But which nation?' The students massed in front of the old Congress Building must have asked that question amongst themselves as the president's words boomed from the huge speakers outside the building.

They were all there, the students from Manila's exclusive Catholic universities for the elite, the boys in thick eyeglasses, long-sleeved white cotton shirts, psychedelic ties running down their chests. The girls also came, in their white blouses and blue dresses cut above the knees. For this 'out-of-school activity', they had asked their housemaids to fold and resew their hemlines the night before, so they could bare more legs.

There were also students from Manila's boisterous diploma mills. Boys in their Beatles haircut, Vonnel V-necked shirts, and tight double-knit pants. The girls came in bright minis that stopped a throb away from their knickers.

Above these young people bloomed the banners of protest, the boom of voices that began being raised five years earlier, when President Lyndon B. Johnson dropped by Manila en route to Saigon, to finalize plans to pulverize North Vietnam. They were only less than a hundred, then, my mother told me, students carrying banners with the words: '*LBJ, LBJ, how many babies did you kill today?*'

However, now they numbered in the thousands, their ranks swelling with the labourers from the working-class districts of Quiapo, Santa Cruz and Tondo and by students from Southern Luzon. Ranged against them were the cops in khaki uniforms and the soldiers in green, bristling with wooden sticks, truncheons and shields.

As the president spoke of another country (less crime, more exports, a vibrant democracy), the young firebrands also worked the crowd. One leader of the nationalist Left, who needed no beer to unloosen his tongue, carped against the rich: 'The rich wear perfumes that they store in gallons and have underwear of silk. We only have the detergent Tide and our underwear are recycled from cotton sacks that used to contain chicken feed.'

Then the doors of Congress opened. First came the secretaries, the undersecretaries, the assistant secretaries and their manifold assistants – the cockroaches, the crows and the centipedes. They were followed by the president, with eyes like a pig's, his face turning greasy with the years. And like Lady Macbeth, there was the First Lady, with her big and lacquered hair adorned with a diamond comb, her neck laced with an intricate string of rubies the colour of blood, her bosom heaving, overflowing with love for the wretched of the earth.

Then from the student's ranks someone threw a crocodile made from carton, right at the direction of the First Couple. The president and the First Lady ducked just in time to avoid being grazed by the crocodile's teeth. Their military escorts shielded them and herded them past the crowd, and they soon vanished inside their stretch black limousine.

After this, the *Free Press* said, came the madness.

The police and the military put on their black masks and began to lob canisters of tear gas into the air, in the direction of the protesters. Then they swooped down on the students, their wooden sticks and trenches swinging wildly. They bashed heads; they shattered arms and knees. You could hear the bones breaking. In turn, the students threw rocks and Molotov cocktails, heaping a rain of curses on the cops and the soldiers. The police then retorted with snake-shaped cannons whose water came from Manila's filthy canals. Coils of brackish water were trained on the students' ranks, who held forth, one arm linked to each other, forming a seemingly impregnable human shield. In time the shield cracked. The students broke ranks and only ran away when the military began to shoot with live bullets.

As dusk fell, shadows ran only to be mowed down by the bullets. Like a tangled net, the screams rose in the hot and humid air. Some students managed to run all the way to Mendiola Street, cross the bridge and gather in front of the president's Malacañang Palace. They commandeered a fire truck, drove it straight back up, once, twice, thrice – and then the tall, iron gate gave way, the students spilt over onto the grounds, jumping with jubilation, only to be cut down by a hail of bullets from the marines. Their sharp eyes picked out their targets as if they were in a shooting gallery during a Christmas fair. Those who did not fall began to run, with the marines chasing them, driving the students toward the other direction, at street's end, where barbed wires, row upon row of the rustiest wires, awaited them.

And so it was that the students who were running away saw before them the barbed wires arrayed like black teeth. Some of them did turn around and raise their hands. The smell of gunpowder and blood was already in the air. The marines cocked their rifles, took aim and then shot the students one by one. Seeing these, the other students just ran and ran in the direction of the barbed wires, then jumped blindly on to them, their elbows raised like wings.

C-47

In that moment floating between wakefulness and dream, I first smelt the crushed garlic. Its heady, golden-brown fragrance sizzled in the morning air and I finally tugged myself from the depths of a dream. I knew that Ludy would be frying again last night's rice in that lake of garlic and vegetable oil, then season it with sea salt. I rubbed my knuckles against my eyes to wipe away the cobwebs of sleep, stepped out of the room and saw Mama in the dining room.

'Oy, wash your face now so we can have breakfast,' she said, dressed in her sky-blue teacher's uniform.

'Where's Ludy?' I asked.

'As usual, she must be taking her sweet time buying bread from the bakery in the street corner,' Mama said.

Before she could recite a litany of other complaints, I had gone to the bathroom. I turned the faucet on. The cold water tightened the skin on my hands. I washed my face.

I heard the familiar sound of our jeep. I quickly dried my face, then ran to the front door and opened it.

I reached only up to Papa's belly, which spilt generously from his black leather belt. Too much beer, Mama would often say, in a tone hovering between a complaint and a declaration. To which Papa would only answer with a grunt.

But this morning, when I raised my face, I saw a strange paleness on Papa's face.

'C'mon, Danny Boy, let's have breakfast now. I'm in a hurry,' he said, then walked quickly to Mama. They talked briefly, in hushed tones, and then I think I heard Mama stifle a sob.

After breakfast, Papa cleared his throat. When I looked at his eyes, I knew something was wrong.

He said, 'A C-47 plane crashed in the town of Lubao an hour ago. I heard it from the commissary. The passengers are now being evacuated to the hospital.'

When I looked at Mama, she seemed to wilt in her uniform. Her shoulders were hunched and her eyes were lined with red. Papa stood up and turned his face away. In a bitter voice he said, 'That C-47 plane should have been thrown to the junk ages ago!'

Sweat began to break on my back, even if it was a cool morning. I ran after Papa who was already out of the house.

As I sat beside Papa in the jeep, I felt the morning like a cold knife against my skin. It was already March and summer was about to begin, but the wind gusting from the Zambales mountain range made the mornings still shivery. The sun was still rising, balancing itself on the mountains. And the rest of the military airbase was still asleep.

We reached the main road that forked in two directions. On the left it swerved to the main road hemmed in by big acacias and white buildings. On the right, the road led to the small, well-equipped hospital. Papa stopped the jeep. I got off, intending to kiss him goodbye.

Just then, the siren of an ambulance broke the early morning silence. Papa and I looked to the left almost at the same time. An ambulance loomed, its siren screaming. It sped past us, then wound its way into the hospital's driveway. It screeched to a halt before the lobby.

Papa restarted the engine of the jeep and I climbed back on the front seat. In a few seconds, we reached the lobby just as the ambulance doors were beginning to open.

A hospital attendant in green cotton uniform got out, then lifted a stretcher whose other end was carried by another attendant. I saw the face of Papa's friend, the one who loved to play chess under the star-apple trees in our backyard, his eyes alive to the pieces on the board, plotting the moves in his mind. But now his eyes were shut. His khaki uniform was torn to shreds around the elbows and knees.

'Pablo!' Papa shouted as the attendants rushed back to the ambulance. The next stretcher carried Mrs Medina, Mama's friend. Her body was limp, as if all of her bones had turned to water. Blood clotted on her white dress.

Another ambulance siren wailed. Just then, I felt something huge and burning in my stomach. Bile rose to my throat, flooding my tongue. I shut my eyes and when I opened them, I saw my vomit through a film of tears. Papa bent down, then wiped my eyes and lips quickly with his handkerchief. He led me away, back to our jeep, back to home.

I had fever on and off for several days. I could only sleep when my eyelids had become as heavy as stones. In one of my dreams, broken glass panes tried to hold themselves together, their patterns shaped like cobwebs. Then when they could no longer hold back, the veins of glass finally burst, turning everything into blood . . .

By day, I began reading *King Arthur and the Knights of the Round Table*, which Papa had long wanted me to read. I was sick; I marked the pages where Merlin, the magician, appeared. After closing the book, I would sometimes scan the white ceiling, wishing I could talk to Merlin. I wanted to ask him if he could erase bad memories?

Luis visited me and filled me in on the lessons I had missed. He also told me the latest funny anecdotes in class. He would sit on the rocking chair from across my bed and talk endlessly to cheer me up, until it was time for dinner. He would then go to the kitchen, and return with a tray containing my food. He would also get another tray and take his dinner with me. My liking for Luis sharpened because of his solicitousness and care: he was always there when I was ill, or weak, or just wanted company. Sometimes we went to his house and climbed the fruit trees in their yard. We would just sit there, together, on the sturdy branches, eating the sun-ripened guavas, the green leaves and the blue sky embracing us.

Luis was like my shield, my safe and secret shield.

When I went back to school, the accident still burnt on the lips of my classmates. They brought to school copies of the *Manila Times*, which had bannered the news on its front pages. *Forty-five killed in Pampanga plane crash*, the headline said. I turned away from my classmates, thinking that those were mere words: they did not capture that morning's terror.

After the lunch break, my classmates talked about the wake. The countless stands of frangipani flowers smothered the chapel such that some of them were already displayed outside. A young man just stood quietly for days beside the coffin of his girlfriend, all of eighteen years old. Children with black ribbons pinned on their shirts roamed in the chapel and the grounds, wondering aloud when Daddy would wake up from his sleep. And then, my classmates talked about the dead, their faces locked in pain, this woman whose limbs were found hanging from a nearby tree, that soldier whose balls were crushed . . .

Papa and Mama did not bring me to the chapel, or raise the topic of the accident in my presence. Even Ludy had been ordered to keep quiet. I knew they must have slipped into the chapel when

I was asleep. They must have even gone to the mass burial, but I never saw them grieving again, until I looked at their eyes and saw everything there.

When I returned to school, my classmates badgered me about my unusual silence. They asked me if I was there in the chapel as well, brave enough to look at the faces of the dead.

'No,' I answered. 'I stayed at home because of my tonsillitis.'

The Kite

The days went by. The wind began to die amongst the acacia leaves shrouding our house. And the heat, ahhh, the heat became so fierce it gave me headaches.

At noon, when I squinted, I could see the heat waves writhing like small liquid snakes in the air. I kept to myself, catching up with the lecture notes that Luis had lent to me. When graduation day came, I was quite disappointed, because I only got the Second Honours. Maria Theresa—a tall, lovely girl with a black mole like a five-centavo coin on her right cheek—got the First Honours. Anyway, I'll study harder in Grade Six, I thought. And besides, it was already summer. I knew I could roam everywhere with my friends, with no thought of the assignments I had to do for next day's classes.

During the days, my friends and I played with marbles the colours of a peacock's tail. Sometimes, my friends spun their wooden tops, and I could only stare at them with savage envy as they threw their wooden tops on the ground. The tops would spin with such grace and speed for all the world to see—a whirl of wood and light and air! And then, my classmates would lasso the tops and throw them right in the middle of their palms: the tops would still be alive and spinning in a blur.

When I did that, my wooden top would wobble on its tiny pointed toe, and just drop dead.

When night fell, we had mock war battles with the boys from the other side of the river. We used slingshots for weapons. For bullets, we used clay pellets or dried papaya seeds. Luis and I always belonged to the same group. I thought of ourselves as Batman and Robin. Together now and forever, for all time. Sometimes, we would hide behind the trunk of the giant acacia tree, our bodies pressed close together I could smell the fragrance of soap on his skin, or feel his arm warm against mine. And then, the cicadas would begin their one-note singing, a rich, heavy sound that would sift through the trees and float to the nearby homes, warm with light and the smell of dinner. I always felt safe and invincible when I was with Luis. I wish I could be with him until we grow old.

Sometimes, my friends and I played hopscotch or hide-and-seek, hiding behind the trees, in the pigsty, or near the bamboo cages inside which the chickens, disturbed, would cackle. And when the chaser would be near any of us, we would run away, our shadows breaking the moonlight. After this game of hide and seek, the winners' shrill voices rose in the air, and in the night sky, the stars of summer shuddered.

One afternoon, we decided to make our own kites. We teased the younger kids in the block who only knew *bôka-bôka,* the kites made of grade-school pad paper, with folded edges for wings and broomsticks for ribs. We, the older ones, used split bamboo for our kites. For the bodies and heads, we used thin paper that was made in Japan and that came in different colours. For the tails, we used long *crêpe* paper, a kind of tissue paper that was creased to make for a crinkly texture. Then we glued powdered bits of glass on the thread, so the thread could easily cut the opponents' thread.

'Let's play in the field near Gate One,' Eduardo said. 'I'm tired of running around in the fields behind our houses.'

At twelve years old, he was the oldest and the biggest in our group, and therefore, the unofficial boss. This claim was confirmed in an unspoken manner early that summer, when he boasted that he had just been circumcised by Old Damaso, the barber, in the woodlands near the river. Old Damaso chewed the tender guava leaves while he cut Eduardo's foreskin with a razor blade. Afterward, the old man spat his saliva on his hand and put the saliva around the wound. He then asked Eduardo to take a plunge in the clear water. Eduardo, the now-circumcised Eduardo, also led our group in stealing the red watermelons from the fields of our neighbour, Thomas. Sure, our parents could afford those sweet, succulent fruits. But somehow, stolen watermelons seemed sweeter.

'Yes, let's do that. The fields there are wider, and the wind, stronger,' said Enrique, his voice always hoarse, as if he had sung all night.

I felt my heart beat furiously. I remembered that the wreckage of the C-47 plane had been towed from its crash site to Gate One. 'For investigation,' said the official reason but my friends and I knew it was there because the people outside the military airbase would have pried the wreckage apart, then sold it per kilo to the nearest junk dealer.

'Okay, let's go,' Luis pressed on.

I thought: If I don't come with them, they'll ask why. They'll know and then they would call me a sissy. 'Okay, let's go,' I heard myself say, in a full-bodied voice that seemed not to belong to me.

The sun was hiding behind a belly of clouds when we reached the dirt road beside the fields. When the wind blew, the white feathery flowers of the cogon grasses began to ripple, like so many waves.

'The wind here's really stronger,' said Eduardo.

Enrique smiled smugly, glad that he had been proven correct.

'O, let's have a dogfight now!' Eduardo continued.

'Yes, now! Now!' came their cry, which became louder and louder as they geared their kites for battle.

I looked at my kite: a red head, blue body, and white tail. It even had the tricolour of the Philippine flag! I noticed only now, and I smiled. I had worked on it for two straight days, buying the materials with the coins I had saved and kept in an empty can of Darigold milk. I had with my own hands cut the bamboo from the grove near the river, then split it with my father's machete. Afterward, I whittled the wood to the shape of the kite's ribs. When everything was ready, I pasted the *papel de japon* on the ribs of my kite, body and bone becoming one.

Even if I lose, I thought, I'll still keep *my* kite.

I released some line from the ball of thread in my hand. And then I ran on the dirt road, following my friends who were running ahead of me. Our thin cotton shirts began to fill with the wind, like sails billowing.

The kites of Enrique and Luis rose slowly but with majesty in the air. The heads of their kites bumped again and again. The threads entwined, trying to cut each other. Finally, Luis's thread snapped, and his kite went veering to the left. Luis ran after it.

'*Al-agua! Al-agua!*' the boys chorused, their words rising in the air, in memory of the kite games of old done on white sandy beaches, when the kites had to be saved from certain destruction if they fell without grace into the sea.

Eduardo and I were the opponents, and this early, I was not sure of my chances. Eduardo's kite was bigger, but I knew that my thread was certainly sharper and stronger.

Our kites soared slowly in the blue enamel of the sky. I felt the wind becoming heavy on the line of my thread. Cheers rose around us while the heads of our kites tried to smash each other's body, cut each other's tail. On and on it went for minutes, the kites circling each other, bumping, and then smashing against each other: gladiators on the kill.

With a sudden and strong tug at my kite, I finally ripped Eduardo's. But his kite swung back, his thread entwining itself around my thread. Then suddenly, I felt the wind's pull beginning to go from my line. When I squinted, I was horrified to see my kite falling in a wide, aimless arc.

My kite drifted away, borne by the wind in the direction of the cogon grasses. I ran after it, my ears filling with the sound of the boys' voices: 'Al-agua! Al-agua!'

Everything was green and sharp. I used my arms to ward off the stalks of tall cogon that were blocking my path. The flowers smothered me, filling my nose and mouth with the spores hidden inside the thin, light strands.

Something warm began to trickle from my left arm, but I did not stop to look at it.

I only wanted to save my kite but something in the middle of the field cut the light. Its swift and sharp reflection bounced back to me. My kite had fallen near the wreckage of the C-47 plane, now a mass of twisted aluminium and steel.

My heart boomed. When I looked down, there were threads of blood on my left arm. For a moment, I just stood there without moving, not knowing what to do.

Slowly, I went to my kite. I bent down and picked it up. I thought it would have a hole, but it looked just the way it did before. It was still whole.

Suddenly, the wind blew. It sounded like a moan, like somebody in the throes of pain. The cogon lifted their stalks and flowers to the wind, heaving wildly, loudly, about me. I began to sweat. I began to call for Luis . . .

But nothing else happened.

Years later, I would know that what I had heard, if anything, was the sound of something fleeing from me. On that day, in the middle of the field, standing beside the plane's wreckage, I could only grip my kite—solid, whole, almost pure—gripping it like a shield against the wilderness of the wind.

The Freak Show

The field of grass between the commissary and the school would be fenced off a week before the eighth of May. Then we knew it was time for the *perya*, the carnival which was always the centrepiece of our fiesta.

My neighbours and I would be there, amongst the bright and multi-coloured lights, the endless rides and games. There would be the rollercoaster and the carousel, the Giant Woman Who Eats Live Chickens and the Hairy Giant from the Deepest Jungle of Borneo.

On the night of the fiesta I took the Ferris wheel with Luis, and in that spinning cage I felt my heart throbbing. *Whoosh* went the sound of the big wheel, and soon our cage was on top of the world, rocking slowly to and fro. In front of us, the dark Zambales mountains brooded. Above us shone the light of so many dead stars. A wind blew, and something stirred in me as I gripped the cold iron bars. I wanted to touch Luis's hand, which was so very near me, or his thigh, which was warm beside my thigh. I wanted to touch them and not these cold iron bars. But I did not dare do any of that. I felt an access of sadness as I just sat there, feeling alone in the empty air, even if my dearest Luis sat close to me. When the ride ended, Luis and I walked round and round the perya.

Of course, we did not walk with our hands locked together—even if I ached to do so.

Yes, the queens were also back from last year's performance and they were not a drag. Tall and willowy, lovely in their red minis and black bustiers, they had come to paint the town flamingo-pink.

Shirley Bassey sang of the most intense love in the *karera ng daga*, the race of the hamster. The handsomest boys at the base ogled her, hooted and whistled as Shirley Bassey did the torch. The queen just batted her mile-long eyelashes, pouted those lips shiny with glitter, and threw kisses at the boys.

Luis and I just stood there, at the back, following with our eyes the hamster running and running in the tracks, finally stopping before a number. Whatever item (plastic pail, a deck of cards, a small mirror) was attached to the number went to the lucky person with that number. And in between the heats of this rat race, Shirley Bassey and Diana Ross and Dionne Warwick— the queens of high cheekbones—serenaded us with torch songs, pouted marvellously, and pulled on the straps of their black bras.

I deliberately ignored them, because Papa had told me to avoid them because they were freaks. Once, my father even scolded me for walking with my books held close to my chest. 'You should walk with your chest out, your stomach in and your gaze level in the distance,' he told me once. 'This is the way boys should walk.' He had also sketched my life for me—university studies at a good school in Manila, a programme of study on Business Management, followed by Law School at either the University of the Philippines or Saint Ignatius University, a master's of Law on scholarship at an American university, then back to the Philippines to work my way up in the corporate canyons of Makati's Central Business District. This was the arc of his dreams for me.

When school opened again in June, all the boys in Practical Arts class crowded around Ernie, who said he was in the perya with one of the general's sons.

Paco was 18, and he was a gorgeous brat with his deep dimples, strong jawline and penetrating eyes. That night in May his hair was tousled; he was freshly bathed and was wearing his tight jeans when I saw him and his friends stop before Shirley Bassey, who was wearing a red feather boa and a black mermaid dress with silver sequins like so many small moons. She immediately locked eyes with Paco. In turn, the gorgeous brat smiled, Ernie said, showing his deep dimples.

After the show, Paco went to the back door of the rat-race stall and talked to Shirley Bassey, whose real name was Horace Saturnino Botictic. A deal was struck and later that night, Shirley Bassey found herself the happiest person in the world. And what on earth did they do?

'Oh,' Ernie said. 'Shirley went down on him to blow him.' I then waited for him to tell us what it meant. Shirley did not really blow Paco's dick. She licked and nibbled and sucked, but she never blew. And like the future president of the greatest country in the world, she blew but she never swallowed.

I turned away and thought, to blow? Won't it tickle you so? The mouth turning into wind? Into the shape of the letter *O*?

How Does One Fall in Love?

Luis was my 'seat mate' in Grade One. He sat on my left while Vivian sat on the right. Even on the first few days of school, I was already confused. I liked Vivian; she was tall and bright and kind, even if she had scabies on her legs, pink raised bumps with a clear top filled with fluid. But I also liked Luis. Not only was he tall and bright and kind, there was also an almost electric energy around him that I felt whenever I saw him.

When I was in Grade One, I didn't know what it was called. Just that I wanted to be with him in gardening class, drawing water from the pond in front of the principal's office, then watering our garden plots bursting with the leaves of *pechay* and appendages of eggplants. Just that I wanted to stare at him when he recited in class, giving the square roots of numbers and answering questions in multiplication with almost the speed of light. Or so I thought, being in that state between admiration and levitation. Just that I wanted to walk with him on the way home, looking at the playground swarming with children, the commissary filling up with customers in the late afternoon, the cogon grasses beginning to flame with sunset's vermilion and gold.

He was the last person I thought of before I slept, Luis of the smooth skin and the face aureoled with light. And he was the first person I thought of upon waking up, making up scenes in my mind about how the weekday would turn out. Or if it was a Saturday, I would invite Luis for a game of pelota in the court beside the humongous hangar, then we would have snacks of *hopia*, thin flaky pastry filled with purple yam, and soda in the commissary while around us, the small, pink flowers of the acacia fell, one by one.

The Initiation

The crisp early morning air made me shiver as I stepped out of our house. The sky was smooth and white like an eggshell.

I walked, gripping my black imitation-leather bag full of new hardbound books and spiral notebooks. Beyond the cogon loomed the commissary, a series of buildings that formed the letter *L*. Streaks of white and blue blurred before my eyes. Maybe my classmates are also excited, I thought, on this, the first day of classes. My strides became longer and faster when I remembered that Don Bosco Academy in Bacolor, the private high school where I was enrolled, was 30 kilometres away.

All the shops were still boarded up when I reached the commissary. Some of the boys sat on the concrete benches; others loitered about, displaying their new black leather shoes. Three of them stared at me. Or rather, *glared* at me. I walked slower, deciding where to wait for the school bus, suddenly conscious of my new white polo shirt with its crisp collar and my new double-knit pants, their elephant bottoms so wide they could even sweep the floor clean.

I met their gaze squarely, my eyes travelling from their faces to their hands: no bags, not even a single spiral notebook. I bit my lower lip.

I sat on a bench, crossed my legs, and put my bag on my lap, defiantly. From the corner of my eyes, I saw the three boys exchanging amused glances.

On my left stood the huge acacia, its pink flowers like a carpet on the ground. Luis would come from this direction.

Only Luis and I could study in Don Bosco Academy: some could not afford it; others flunked the entrance exams, while the parents of some feared that the men from the hills would swoop down on the busload of students, sons of soldiers in the base, and hold us hostage.

Finally, Luis arrived at 6.15 a.m. I marked the time on my black *Casio*, a gift from my father because I had graduated as the class valedictorian. I thought my friend looked different now: in his new high-school uniform, he was already a young man. A small pimple even bloomed on his right cheek. Luis's hair still dripped from his morning bath. And he also did not bring any bag or notebook with him. I wanted to tell Luis to dry the beads of water sliding down his cheeks, but I was still annoyed.

'Why didn't you tell me we're not supposed to bring our things today?' I asked, rising from the bench to meet him.

The smile from Luis turned into a grin when he saw my things. Then he said sheepishly, 'I'm sorry. I wasn't able to go to your house over the weekend. I should have told you the first day is just the orientation day. We have to bring our things on the second day.'

I just smiled at him, although what I really wanted to do was to spank him.

The rumble of the bus cut our conversation short. The bus stopped beneath the shadows cast by the acacia. Along the length of its body ran the tawny stripes of a tiger. On top of the stripes, ARMED FORCES OF THE PHILIPPINES was spelt out in white paint.

We all rushed for the door. The upperclassmen began teasing Sergeant Molina, the escort, with easy familiarity. 'Oh, it's you again, Sarge?' they said, slapping his shoulders and tugging at the broad black strap of his Armalite. An ammunition belt bristling with bullets the size of thumbs was wound around his waist.

'Hurry up,' he said through teeth with the shape and colour of corn ears. 'Traffic might be heavy again in Guagua.'

The moment I stepped inside the school bus I noticed the young driver: his crew cut showed a strong neck. He had wide shoulders, his body forming the letter V, and his buttocks filled the seat of his khaki pants.

The Salesian Brother who led the singing of the national anthem looked as if he had just come out of a closet: His cassock hung from his shoulders that were as thin as a clothes hanger.

'Please form a line,' he said while raising his hand to silence us. 'You will first attend the Holy Mass, which you'll do every morning. Then you will go to your rooms for the orientation day. You will also have a diagnostic test.' A murmur broke amongst the students at the word *test*.

The chapel was badly lit and the sermon, abominably long. What kept me going was the sight of the glass windows: when the sunlight touched them, the window panes simply bloomed. Jesus, Mary and Joseph sprang to life, the reds and blues of their robes vibrant, shimmering between the sunlight outside and the chapel's dark interiors.

After the Holy Mass, I followed the other 1-A students to the classroom. A small, balding man with lidless eyes slouched near the door. The skin around his neck was loose, like that of a turtle's.

After the last student had stepped inside the room, the teacher went inside and walked to the platform. 'Okay, please be seated.

I'm Mr Baltazar, your English teacher,' he said in a voice that came from his noise.

I sat on the second row, not in front: I sensed my teacher was the type who would send a shower of saliva when he spoke. Besides, I noticed that my eyes were beginning to go bad. Must be from reading my father's *Penthouse* at sundown, before he came back from work.

'Please pass this around,' Mr Baltazar said, handing a bundle of mimeographed paper to the students in front of him. 'This is just a diagnostic test to gauge your skills in English.' Then his eyes lit up: 'Those who graduated from this school, please raise your hands.' Almost half of the students did. 'Good, I'm sure you'll find this test very easy.' He paced the platform, an actor conscious of his blocking. Then he added, 'I'm sure that those who came from public schools will find this test really difficult.'

The school was built like a fortress. Its cemented walls were grey and tall and thick, their tops spiked with glass shards and nails, with the pointed tips upward. Outside the school a group of shanties leaned on the walls. Below the shanties, the ground seemed perpetually under water. The shanties seemed to tremble as our school bus sped past them.

Mount Arayat rose on the horizon. The sugar cane fields had been burnt to the ground after the cane had been cut, to fertilize the earth. Every summer, Luis and I would sneak out of the military airbase and hide in the dry canal beside the road. We would throw stones at the trucks loaded with the cut sticks of sugar cane. When the truck stopped, we would run to its back, pull a stick of sugar cane, and then run back to the canal. We did all this in a few seconds, such that when the driver had slid down the truck, he would find nobody around. And since the sugar mill waited for no man, he would curse us, the hooligans he knew were just hiding around. *'Your mothers are whores.'* Then he would return morosely to the truck and leave. Luis and I would gleefully suck on the sticks of sugar cane, all that burst of liquid sweetness dripping down our fingers, down our chins.

After the sugar cane had been harvested, the farmers outside the military airbase would then plant rice. In a few days, the rice fields would begin to turn green. Men and women would transfer the saplings from seedbed to field. I wondered how it must have hurt the body, bending in that arc for a long time, with the sun flagellating their backs.

Suddenly, I remembered my father. We were on a train bound for Albay, passing by a scene straight out of a painting by Fernando Amorsolo: the rice fields amazing in the golden ripeness of their grain. Father told me he used to help in the rice fields when he was a kid. 'My eyes had to be really sharp so I could spot the grains that fell on the ground, son.'

After that, I took pains to finish *all* the morsels of rice that Ludy set before me, especially when my father was there. Not out of a sense of duty, I told myself, but out of a sense of pain, for my father had told me these stories again and again, especially on those nights when he would go home drunk, a dark and bitter edge in his voice as he told me about escaping from the barrio to try his luck in the city, working as a newspaper boy and a bootblack to support himself through public high school, and later, getting a scholarship at the Philippine Military Academy and then, finally, the Air Force Academy at Colorado Springs in the United States.

When I was growing up, my father took evening classes in Guagua for an undergraduate degree in political science. After getting that degree, he continued studying for a degree in Law, tangling with the thorny texts of the *Revised Penal Code,* Books One and Two, and getting lost in the slippery labyrinths of statutory construction.

My father had wanted me to study in this Catholic high school, although it was far and expensive. He even went with me on the day I took the examinations. He waited outside the classroom for two hours while I answered all the questions. He was also there when I got the results: number two among more than 1,000 applicants. I had wanted to tell Papa I might not finish in Don Bosco Academy in Bacolor. Papa would soon resign from the military to work as an engineer with Lockheed in Saudi Arabia. He would leave in September.

'The government is a thankless employer, son. The pay is very low, that's why I've to leave, but don't worry. You'll still study in a good private school when we move to Quezon City. You can transfer to Don Bosco Mandaluyong by September. I want you to have the best . . .' We were walking down the long driveway fringed with big acacias whose leaves and branches interlaced overhead, forming the green dome of a cathedral. It was a long walk toward the tall and ornate gate. Later, we would go to San Fernando and Papa would treat me to *pancit luglug*, the noodles neither limp nor hard, the bits of pork skin just fried to the right crispness, the red-orange sour-sweet shrimp sauce made more savoury by a lemony dash of calamansi.

L uis whispered something in my ear, but I could not make out his words. The wind in the highway leapt from the window and lashed our faces. 'What did you say?'

'The initiation,' he said, his eyes shifting. 'The upperclassmen in this bus have an initiation for us freshmen.'

Suddenly, Ricky, who sat behind the driver stood up. He had three chins and a nose scarred with pimples. He was the son of the second highest officer in the base. This brat laughed at his lewd jokes, followed by the canned laughter coming from his friends.

I heard Luis heave a sigh when Ricky walked past us and sat beside Eddie, the mayor's son. Eddie was a tall, handsome boy whose singular embarrassment was his mother. Every morning, the school bus would stop in front of their gate. Eddie would run out of their mansion, followed by his mother, her hair a peroxide blonde, and her reminder—'Don't forget to drink this milk!'— then handling him a jug.

'That Ricky,' said Luis, jerking his thumb backward, 'leads the rites.'

The next morning, Mr Baltazar looked wilted in his chair. 'I'm disappointed,' he said, raising the test papers. The class began to buzz.

'Ferdie, what happened to you?' the teacher asked, rising from his chair. 'You were the grade-school valedictorian of Don Bosco, but you only got an 85.'

I shifted uneasily in my seat.

'Danilo Cruz,' the teacher said, casting a glance across the room.

'Yes, sir?' I said, raising my hand.

'You got 90, the highest. Did you graduate from Sacred Heart Academy?'

I rose from my chair to get back my paper. As I did so, I took in a gulp of air. From up close, Mr Baltazar looked so vulnerable. I could not help it, and so I said, 'No, sir. I came from Basa Central Elementary School. It *is* a public school.'

My teacher was a good actor and his face did not betray any emotion, but as I walked back to my seat, I knew he was pissed.

The twelve o'clock bell rang, a shrill sound that cut the heat into fragments.

Ahead of our classmates, Luis and I had gone to the cafeteria. Housemaids in their white, starched uniforms and drivers in their stiff visors wandered about, bringing the lunch of Pampanga's

Little Lord Fauntleroys. One of my classmates, Van Go, had several watches, and I asked him why. He looked at me and snapped, 'Danny, there are seven days in a week!' This was also the boy who, when asked to write a theme paper called "How I Spent My Summer Vacation", wrote how he got lost in London's exclusive Knightsbridge, because the housemaid took a long time in the loo, and he began to walk around the borough. I wished he were never found.

I sat down on a chair beside a screened window. Luis put down his things on a chair and bought our bottles of soda.

Below the cafeteria stretched the glassy blueness of the swimming pool. Suddenly I wished I could take a dip because the noon heat was unbearable. But the sign said that only the Salesian Brothers and physical education students could use the pool.

Luis returned with one soda that was almost chilled (his) and another that was not even cold (mine). My mother had fixed for me my favourite: chicken *tocino* and big, ripe tomatoes. I was about to have lunch when Luis leaned closer.

'Do you know what happens in the initiation?' he asked.

'Oh, no, not again,' I said. 'Who's been telling you these stories?'

'Elmer, the sophomore who lives near my house. He said it's usually done behind the gym.'

I remembered I had been there once—a wooded area where the interlacing leaves of the mahogany trees virtually shut out the sun. The brothers had told us not to go behind the gym because snakes had been spotted there.

The voice of Luis broke into my thoughts. 'And there are different ways of going about it.'

'Oh, *really?*' I said, deciding to get into what I had dismissed as a game.

'One is they ask you to buy a pack of Marlboro. Then they'll order you to smoke the whole pack, alone, in an hour. Just to prove them you're already a man.'

'What if you can't?'

'Well, if you can't, they'll light the remaining sticks and stub them all out. On your thighs and buttocks, where nobody can see them. Elmer showed me his burnt scars. Very black, even after a year. Of course, there are other ways . . .'

The food began to feel like stones in my throat.

A Burning in the Air

That afternoon, the school bus left without Ricky. His friend, Eddie, told the driver that Ricky had already gone home ahead of us.

Ay, the stories of Luis, I thought as I lifted the glass windows and set the side locks in place. I hope he's just pulling one of his tricks again. I had a low threshold for pain. All my life I would always carry a small plastic bag full of medicines—Tylenol and Imodium, Bonamine and Alaxan, Band-Aid and a host of antibiotics—afraid of dying of one ailment or another.

I recalled I was five years old at the time. My parents had just arrived from work. I was sitting on the stairs, waiting for them. The moment I saw them enter the gate, I ran down the stairs but tripped on the last step and fell, scraping the skin on my knees. Blood flowed. Merthiolate dabbed on the raw wound, bandages smothering me, even in my sleep. Pain like no other, or so I thought.

For now, though, only this wind. I looked at Luis, sitting calmly beside me. He seemed to be changing, stepping into the body of a young man: the hint of hair above the lips, the voice that was beginning to crack, the eyes now both familiar and strange. I loved the warmth when my elbow came close to his elbow, my hand beside his hand. And his lips, how would it feel to kiss those lips?

The wind rose, bearing with it the scent of rice saplings standing above the muddy fields. I wondered how deep the saplings' roots were, how they went about groping for direction, for certainty, in the earth's moist darkness.

Our school bus slowed down when we reached the rotunda at the Guagua *plaza*. Once more, the fire-blackened ruins of an old school rose before us. The bus stopped in front of a restaurant whose walls screamed with neon-green gashes and violet polka dots. The young soldier who drove the bus got off to buy food, while Sergeant Molina told everybody he would just get his laundry from his sister's house on the next street.

I would have taken a quick nap but for the sight of Ricky cutting across the plaza. The black ruins of the school framed him. It must have been caused by the sun, I thought, when I noticed the flush on Ricky's face.

The door of the school bus flew open and Ricky shouted, 'Who told you to leave without me?'

Someone in front volunteered the name. In a flash, Ricky stood before Eddie, aimed his fist and hit Eddie hard on the face. Blood came from a cut on Eddie's lips. In turn, he punched Ricky in the stomach. Ricky fell. The other upperclassmen tried to stop Eddie from lunging at Ricky, who was trying to rise. I stood up and cheered silently for Eddie.

The moment Ricky was on his feet, he shouted: '*Puta!* Your horny father houses his mistress in Porac!'

Eddie's eyes narrowed. Quivering with rage, he said, 'And you, you're like your mother who sleeps with the governor. Why did you sleep with my girlfriend?'

'She seduced me, kid,' Ricky sneered, and then his face twisted into a leer. 'She said she's hot but you haven't even touched her. She even thinks you're a fag, ha-ha-ha!'

Eddie broke free from the hands that restrained him. He surprised Ricky with another jab. Finally, upon noticing the commotion, the young soldier ran out of the restaurant, leapt into the bus, and tried to break up the fight. Both Ricky and Eddie's friends had already joined the melee. A free-for-all erupted.

From the street corner, I saw Sergeant Molina, who dropped his laundry the moment he saw the fight going on inside the bus. He ran inside the bus and shouted, but nobody listened to him. Finally he thrust his Armalite out of the window, and the sound of firing ripped through the darkening afternoon.

It was a cool day. I went back to the school bus parked under a canopy of acacia leaves to get my assignment for social studies—the list of 120 presidents and prime ministers of the world—inside the plastic envelope I had forgotten to bring with me during the morning rush to school.

The school bus was empty. While I was looking for my list of the world leaders, I heard the sound of twigs snapping underfoot. I looked out of the window. The young soldier was walking toward the school bus. Tall, a sensuous spring in his limbs. His skin was as dark as a bar of Cadbury chocolate, which I had begun buying at the cafeteria. Strong, aquiline nose. Bee-stung lips. He continued walking. I thought he would enter the school bus. Instead, he stopped on its side. He unbuckled the stainless-steel clasp of his green belt, pulled down his zipper and began to pee. A crisp stripe of hair ran down his smooth and flat belly. The leaves and the light cast a cool shadow on his navel.

The air began to burn.

The Rites

One Saturday, our homeroom adviser required us to come to school to practise for our presentation in the opening of the sports intramurals. Since Luis had diarrhoea, I took the jeepney all by myself until I reached our school. Our class presentation took the form of an acrostics, with a student holding the blue cut-out of a big letter, then reciting aloud the lines assigned to him. Our section was tasked to spell out several qualities needed in sports, among them F-A-I-R-N-E-S-S, which our teacher said is one quality that our society badly needed. Being the only one in class who did not confuse his *p* with his *f,* unlike the usual residents of our province, I was assigned to deliver the verse for the first letter.

Fairness is what we need
When we play out in the field.
In this way we can have fun
As we frolic in the sun.

I quickly memorized that doggerel, errr, verse, written by our teacher. Wearing my oversized yellow T-shirt, which was the colour of our section, I did deliver the lines with aplomb and was greatly relieved when we were allowed to go home before noon.

After taking my heavy lunch of grilled pork with white rice and tomatoes in the cafeteria, I decided to walk around the campus to let the food settle down in my stomach. I walked around the campus that I would soon leave. I visited the small, black turtle in its pond beside the principal's office. It looked back at me with its sad, lidless eyes, and I silently apologized to it for comparing it earlier to Mr Baltazar. I stopped in the middle of the basketball court, remembering that only yesterday, I stood transfixed as my classmate Randy took off his sweat-soaked shirt, his muscular chest blinding like a shield.

I kept on walking until I found myself near the gym. Prodded by something I could never understand, I walked on the gravel path all the way behind it.

The sudden coolness came from the shadows cast by the giant apitong and narra trees. Shrubs and bushes with their waxen, green leaves enclosed me. Bird calls rose in the air. Deeper and deeper into the heart of the woodlands I walked, until I heard familiar voices.

I hid behind a big acacia tree.

Ricky was there, looming tall in his white T-shirt and white trousers, with the five other sons of the officers in the military airbase. There were four freshmen students in front of them, who took the school bus with me every morning. Suddenly, Ricky kicked the students one by one, hitting them on the thighs, until they fell to the ground. Then the four companions made the freshmen stand up again. Ricky then punched them in the stomach twice, making them wince in pain. Then he punched them on the face, causing a trail of blood to come from their lips. I was trying to breathe as slowly, as inaudibly, as possible.

'What is the Golden Rule, ha? Do you remember?' Ricky asked.

'Do not do . . . unto others . . .what you do not want others . . . to do unto you,' stammered Noel, the tallest amongst the freshmen.

I crouched behind the bushes.

'Good. In short, we must love one another.' He fished for something in his pocket. He showed them to the freshmen. Four candies.

'Before you think we are cruel, we can take a break.' His companions unwrapped the candies, asked the freshmen to open their mouths, and put the candies in the mouths.

'Suck them, and suck them well. Mentholated candies kill the germs in your saliva.' And like canned laughter, Ricky's four companions laughed dutifully.

'And now, since it's very hot, take off your shirts, guys.' The four did as they were told. 'And now, drop your trousers.' The four did not do as told. 'Do you want a kick in the groin?' The four then did as told.

Noel wore white cotton jockeys, while the other three wore nylon ones coloured yellow and blue and brown. The nylon boys' dicks seemed to have shrunk from fear, while Noel's was holding forth with pride and dignity.

'Since we all must love one another,' Ricky said in deep, cathedral tones, 'you will exchange candies with one another.'

But the four did not do as told. 'Or do you want me to order you to do something else?' The four did as told.

'And now, since you have exchanged candies with each other, you might as well exchange salivas, too. You must French-kiss each other!'

The four protested noisily, shaking their heads.

Ricky said, 'Okay, you just failed this initiation rite. Therefore, you will get no leaks for the exams, no pre-written term papers for you, no Betamax tapes, no lending of *Playboy* magazines, no invitation to exclusive parties, no freebies, no friends, nothing!'

'But, Sir,' Noel piped up. 'Could we just do something else?'

'Now that's an idea. Do you want to kiss each other's dicks?'

With big eyes, the three other freshmen looked at each other, and then at Noel.

Noel said, 'Ay, Sir, ummm, we will just, ah, kiss each other on the lips. But is this really the last—'

'Yes, yes,' Ricky answered, with a dismissive wave of his hand. 'But I want you to close your eyes when you kiss each other. And I want to see tongues. This isn't called a French kiss for nothing. And don't you dare stop until I have told you to do so.'

And so the two pairs of freshmen students faced each other. On my haunches, I watched them move their faces close to each other. They opened their lips, drew out their tongues, and kissed clumsily. In the maddening heat of noon, the three nylon boys showed more dignity. But Noel, his stick of sugar cane became a tube, and as he kissed his partner, it grew bigger and bigger by the second . . .

A Season in Hell

In the summer of my twelfth year, I began reading pornography. It was so hot—a season in hell, Rimbaud was right—so I always wore short shorts that summer. I was only twelve years old but I already stood at 5' 4". My legs were long and lean and my arms thin as young bamboo sticks. I went to my neighbour's house to borrow a copy of *Expressweek* magazine. It was the only magazine allowed by the dictatorship to publish, since it was owned by the president's brother-in-law. Every week, it featured, in full and blazing colours, the updated lives of saints. Updated because after these saints had lived and died and had been canonized by the Vatican, their statues made of plaster of Paris were sold throughout the archipelago. The magazine published reports of miracles attributed to kissing the saints' feet: here, a woman was able to walk after being crippled for twenty years; there, a man was gifted with sight after living in darkness for ages.

Saint Peter, who had a large key in one of his hands and a cock, errr, a rooster, in his other hand, had become the patron saint of the cockfighting aficionados. One of them, a burly man by the name of Pedro Pintakasi, knelt before the statue of Saint Peter in his small house atop a hill in Antipolo, jumped aboard a jeepney with his prized rooster, blowing rings of cigarette smoke on the perplexed rooster to prime it up. That rooster had indeed won all its fights, its strong wings a dazzle of feathers blue and red. The small, hooked spur of steel on its left leg glinted. That day, Pedro Pintakasi was joining the major league: the 10-cock grand derby at Araneta Coliseum, that round grey enormity in the middle of Cubao, which was often cited as the largest domed coliseum in the world.

Now the air inside the coliseum had become hot and humid. Pedro's throat was turning dry. He betted everything he had won in the minor leagues—all 50,000 pesos of it—on his rooster. Before he set it down on the ring, the whole coliseum was already in pandemonium, men placing their bets on the roosters, their voices rising to a roar, the Kristo memorizing who had betted how much with whom. If he made a mistake he would pay up, thus suffering miserably. Pedro looked at this rooster nervously. He even talked to it, telling it to go for the kill, or else, it would end up as fragrant chicken *tinola*, with stalks of lemongrass and slices of green papaya, swimming in a soup with crushed ginger and pepper leaves. The losing rooster would end up as that evening's viand in the winner's house.

Pedro Pintakasi did win, and his lucky streak seemed to go on and on that one fine day, Tesoro Barbano, the editor-in-chief of the magazine, assigned his cub reporter Mozart Pastrami to do a 'write-up' of Pedro Pintakasi and his marvellous cock.

And so every Saturday afternoon, I visited the neighbour's house to borrow a copy of their *Expressweek* magazine. On that day, Ate Lina was not there. She had gone to the commissary to buy some provisions. I walked around the living room of their house, but I did not see *Expressweek* magazine but something else instead. Glossier cover, with a photograph of a woman that, as my classmates would put it, had breasts that Tarzan could hang on to for dear life.

I looked around, left, right, in front of me, and back, but there was nobody around. So I sat on the electric-blue sofa and flipped the pages. More photographs of blonde women spilling all of themselves on the glossy pages. I tried to read the stories. 'Virgin Boy' was one of them, about this bored housewife who was left at home, alone, with a hot 'pussy'. I still did not know then what that word meant.

Then one sunny day, she looked out of her window from the second floor of her white house. She saw her neighbour, a young man of seventeen, sunning himself on a white deck chair in their garden. She grabbed a bottle of red wine, asked him to help her unscrew the cork, and when he came to her house, she seduced him.

I felt myself getting a hard-on when she began describing his body: smooth skin and slim waist, a muscular chest beaded with sweat. Later, after she had taken off his clothes, she even described his dick as 'stiff and still hairless' (at seventeen?), the balls moving in their sac when she began to touch them.

I was having a hard-on just reading what she was doing to him and I did not notice *Kuya* Alex, the soldier-husband of Ate Lina, who was already standing behind me. In a flash he was already sitting beside me and then he asked, in his voice that used to be soft but was now harder, breathier, 'What are you doing?' I immediately shut the pages of the magazine. My hard-on vanished.

'Hmmm, reading my copy of *Playboy*, eh?' he asked, his left hand suddenly on my knee, his fingers now like spider legs on my right thigh. I was beginning to be tickled. I felt my bulge coming back. I could feel my heart beginning to beat faster. I was getting excited but I was also afraid. So before his fingers could reach my crotch, I had already stood up, stammered something about getting my siesta, and walked out of the room as swiftly as I possibly could, given the bulge in my shorts.

But before I left their house, I looked at him again when I was near the door. He was looking at me with glazed eyes and slightly parted lips, and then I strode headlong into the mad heat of summer.

Farewell, My Lovely

I sat again on the concrete bench near the acacia, sipping my warm soda and munching *hopia ube,* our favourite pastry. A familiar bicycle—a tall one that I used to call a baker's bicycle— came closer. It was Luis, in khaki shorts and white T-shirt, which I immediately recognized as our uniform in our elementary school. Hair was beginning to grow on his legs. My dearest Luis.

'So you're leaving tomorrow?' he asked.

'Yes,' I said, trying to sheathe my sadness. Then I smiled and said, 'Let me buy you something first.' We went inside the commissary and then came out with a chilled bottle of soda and biscuits. We sat on the benches. The floor was again carpeted with the acacia's pink flowers. Brown acacia pods littered the ground; some of them had already turned into a sticky paste.

I suddenly remembered the cool grotto in Don Bosco, which was also shrouded by ancient acacias. This elevated grotto stood near the wall of the school, over which you could see the big buses passing by, all bound for either Pasay City or Cubao. When my whole family left for Project 4, Quezon City, the month before, I was left to stay with Ludy until our lease in the apartment ran out. So for a whole month, I did not listen to the teacher, but rather drew a rough map of Project 4, Quezon City, marking with orange the new street where we lived. I would have no friends there, but my father said everything would be all right. Still, I felt something, perhaps like a rice sapling being pulled from its seedbed, as I ran down the grotto and returned to the school in the dark afternoon.

'Where will you study now?' Luis asked, making my thoughts scatter.

'The Father Principal has already given me a glowing letter of recommendation for their school in Mandaluyong. I hope it works out fine.'

'You're lucky.'

'Why?'

'Because the initiation will still go ahead.'

'C'mon, don't worry, Luis.' Then I smiled wickedly. 'I wish I could stay here and join you for the initiation.' Luis stared at me, as if I had gone mad. I just ignored him.

Then I asked, 'Could I borrow your bike? I'll just take a spin around the old school.'

That softened him. He smiled sadly. 'Let me come with you, then. For the last time.'

As I began to pedal, Luis jumped on the back seat. 'I wish I could stay here forever,' I said. 'But I can't.' I could feel his breath hot on my nape. I wished he would wrap his arms around me and never ever let go. Pain was like a beast caged in my chest. I wanted to tell him that I liked him, or that I already loved him.

But of course, I never breathed a word to him. Not. At. All.

Part 2

The Country of Dreams

Riverrun

I woke up, on the edges of sleep my slippery dream of Luis. I held the dream close to my chest, so it would burn still.

In my dream Luis seemed to be pierced with light. He was all there, blinding me with his smile, the eyes that were wicked and innocent at the same time. The moustache beginning to grow above his moist and reddish lips.

In my dream Luis was about to say something, some words I would hold on to in the summer of my departure. I would soon leave the province and follow my parents who now lived in Manila—ahhh, mad, maternal Manila. In the fever of a summer afternoon I wanted to store some images and words that would have the weight, the depth, of the first rains of May.

The first rains of May falling in exuberance over the land, a crystalline cascade waking up everything—grass, leaf, sky, even the very air—from the languorous sleep of summer.

A cloud broke open and the rain fell. I savoured the sound of the rain falling. Ludy's ears were glued to the transistor radio, listening to Brother Eddie giving bits of advice to the lovelorn. I dashed out of the house in my white cotton shirt and shorts.

My mother's red roses were crumbling against the white, grainy wall of our house.

The sound of the rain would never leave me, haunting me like a memory I could never bury. It was like a whisper in the ear, a hum growing louder, a roar. In the street corner, under the dripping leaves of the acacias, I stopped.

Luis was running in the rain, naked from the waist up. His nipples were like small, brown berries. His shorts barely concealed his thighs now growing to a fullness. He waved when he saw me, motioning me to come to him. I did, and I took in everything my eyes could hold: a young and beautiful boy glistening in the rain.

Together we ran in the rain, in the summer of our twelfth year, the year I would leave for the city. Everything seemed to be melting, but not me. Warmth ran through my limbs, flowing like blood in my veins. We ran and ran until we reached the river fringed with weeping willows.

'We should swim,' Luis said.

'No,' I answered, 'the river might grow bigger.'

He laughed, and began wading into the water. I was torn between lust and the fear of drowning. Perhaps, I thought at that moment, they're the same?

The river parted, and Luis entered it. I watched him swim, his strokes clean and quick. His buttocks were like islands rising and dipping in the water. I envied the river that tongued his body. I watched him swim farther and farther away from me, until his hair had become one with the sound of the rain.

Stillness

I was alone in my bed, staring at the ceiling. Spots of brown had already formed from the rain that had dried up. Cobwebs that looked like gauze also drooped from the corner of the ceiling.

The ceiling became a map. River, mountain, and hill. Village, town and country. And a face rising to the surface, followed by the echo of a voice.

Luis and I wrote to each other for three months, and then he completely stopped writing. Every afternoon, I waited for the fat, cheerful mailman who woke up the sleepy neighbourhood with the roar of his motorcycle. Upon hearing his motorcycle, I would run to the green gate of our apartment. At first, he said, 'No letter, son.' Afterwards, he would just smile at me and shake his head. I would walk back to our apartment, something grainy in my throat. My eyes scanned the ground for any protruding stone that might stub my toes.

The drowsy summer gave way to the relentless falling of the rain, the season of the terrible typhoons that lashed the archipelago with fury. The rain fell harshly, glinting like the smallest of knives. Still no letter from Luis. The sky turned into lead. The potholes on the road became puddles. The umbrellas turned the air into a madcap of colours.

Still, no letter from Luis.

After Mama arrived from school one afternoon, I asked her, 'Could I visit the military airbase?' She was sitting on our sofa covered with a plastic sheet.

Her left eyebrow arched. 'In the middle of June? With classes just beginning? Perhaps in December, or summer next year.' Then she turned her back and told Ludy to prepare a dinner of glutinous rice flavoured with chocolate and then fry several pieces of dried *danggit* fish.

I walked away from her and locked myself up in the bathroom. The white tiles stared back at me. I touched the wall, spelling out the name of Luis on the white tiles. I touched the tiles as if they were the face of Luis.

The coldness, it just seeped slowly and silently, right through my bones.

How to Survive as a Nouveau Poor

How does a mother survive the nightmare of poverty, or in her case, lower-middle-class poverty?

1. Every morning, she will repeat this line after waking up: 'We're better off than a million others. At least, we have fried fish and tomatoes for breakfast and my husband works as an overseas Filipino worker in Saudi Arabia.' Then she will rise from her bed, wash her face and mouth, proceed to pour vegetable oil into the frying pan. Usually during cool mornings, the lard would have congealed. So, she will get a tablespoon, scoop the lard and let it rest on the bottom of the pan. She will let the lard sputter and quiet down. Now the lard is hot and she can begin frying the dried fish.

2. After frying the fish, she will flatten a head of garlic, slice into small bits, put them into the pan, and then follow this with last night's rice. She will sprinkle salt to taste.

3. She will wake up her only child, now a teenager having his share of sulky days. She will tell him to wash up and then sit before the breakfast table. She will fill his plate with fried rice with garlic enough to last until snack time, then she will give him his allowance of ten pesos per day.

4. She will buy minced meat, not whole slabs of meat. She will use the minced meat sparingly, just enough so that their mung-bean stew would taste of some meat. She will buy a bagful of mung bean, and let a bowl of it stand overnight in water. The bean sprouts will be cooked the next morning, mixed with garlic, onion, tomatoes, soy sauce and calamansi juice.

5. She will look around her workplace to check which item was not yet being sold. In her elementary school, almost everything was already being sold by her fellow public-school teachers: sweetened and caramelized pork meat, Sunday clothes and small, pink angels; insurance plans, funereal services and memorial-park lots. She sold Tupperware, like she did in the 1960s. She felt it was like returning to an old love. Her sales pitch: these lunchboxes would save you money in terms of cheaper, home-cooked food, in the short run, and hospitalization, in the long run: the canteen sells overpriced food filled with cholesterol and salt.

    These plastic glasses can also contain the calamansi juice that you had squeezed right in your very kitchen. No soda, no fake orange flavours, no coffee, no tea: just pure, natural citrus good for bones (ours are beginning to ache from age and this horrible inflation) and teeth (the stronger the better, for the inflation rate would still go up before it went down, and we would need stronger teeth for the chattering to come).

6. On the way home, she would ask for cassava leaves from Mrs Mely who lived around the street corner. Old woman Mely thought her friend would give them to the children in the neighbourhood, to play with. They would break the thin, green-red stems into inch-long strips, the tough skin hanging on, and the strips of stem could be turned into instant necklaces, with the star-shaped leaves as pendant. But no, the cassava leaves could be simmered in coconut milk flavoured

with shrimp paste from Pangasinan. It reminded the mother of what they ate during the darkest days of the Second World War, when they had to flee to the forests to avoid the wrath of the Japanese Imperial Army, with their hobnailed boots and sharp samurais. Her family survived on what they could forage in the heart of the forest: pith of banana trunks and meat of snakes, and yes, cassava leaves simmered in coconut milk, along with small shrimps that used to cluster near the river bank.

7. She would bring home the Nutribuns, those bread hard as rocks that were being distributed to schoolchildren by the Nutrition Foundation under the sponsorship of the First Lady. She would bring these rocks home, use a hammer to pound them down into bits, then soak them in a basin of water. When sufficiently soft, she would pour half the contents of a small can of condensed milk, then add just enough sugar, for sugar was also becoming more expensive now. She would pour the mixture in her old pans, then she would steam the pans. After 30 minutes, she would lift the lid (the steam blurring her very face), set the pans on a basin quarter-filled with water, to cool. Then she would put everything in the refrigerator (heaven help us this fifteen-year-old fridge would not break down, not now, Lord), and the morning after, she would serve this as breakfast to her rebellious teenager, in case he had already gotten tired of having fried fish and fried garlic rice every morning.

8. Night. She would draw a deep, deep sigh. Her husband was working in deepest, hottest Riyadh. The distance would spread between them like a desert. Her heart would thud heavily in her chest.

Then she would repeat numbers one to eight when morning came through, again.

Fourteen

It was a morning without wind. Mrs Santos, our class adviser in II-Narra, walked with me in silence. We were going to the house of Felix, who had been the vice president of our class in first-year high school. Felix was a tall, big-boned boy given to quick smiles and easy laughter. He always wore black leather shoes in school, even on that year when the fad was coloured rubber shoes. He kept his old pair of shoes clean and shining with coat upon coat of inexpensive black dye.

The moment we entered the village of Escopa, I sensed a familiar feeling wash over me: that I was leaving behind a known world, and entering the sad labyrinth of another. On the narrow streets, half-naked children were running after each other, screaming, playing tag or hopscotch, pulling twines tied to the noses of empty sardine cans set on wooden wheels. Fringing the alley were the lean-tos, with their grimy skin of plywood walls, the corrugated-iron roofs held in place by rocks or flat rubber tyres; women in faded floral house dresses washing clothes in the rusty artesian well, or gossiping, or sitting in rows of threes, picking each other's lice; older men fetching water, naked from the waist up, their bloated bellies like the bellies of bullfrogs; some men with multicoloured tattoos of birds and snakes on their biceps and chests, some with tattoos of hearts lacerated by an arrow; younger

men drinking beer at eight o' clock in the morning in front of the
variety store loud with the morning melodrama from the radio,
the men wearing double-knit trousers worn at the knees, several
days' beard and moustache on their faces, their eyes dark and shifty.
And in the air, the heavy smells of the place: uncollected garbage,
brackish water, a stink strong enough to knock you down. But on
and on we walked, into alleys becoming narrower and narrower,
coiling and uncoiling before us, like intestines.

Finally, we stopped before a lean-to set apart from the rest.
'Number 28,' Mrs Santos said, reading the number painted in red
on the wooden wall. Its wooden walls were thin but not dirty; its
angled corrugated-iron roofs were nailed properly into place. A
small crowd had begun to gather inside, but I knew the four thick
wooden posts would hold.

We called out our greetings. A man who must be in his
mid-forties looked out of the window. He nodded in greeting, and
was soon rushing down the stairs.

Our teacher tried to smile. 'Good morning. I'm Mrs Santos,
Felix's teacher and this is Danilo, the president of their class.'

The man who introduced himself as Felix's father nodded and
tried to smile as well. 'Please come in,' he said. He had a firm,
strong face, and skin like wood that had been soaked in the rain
for a long time.

We mumbled our condolences, saying we should have come
yesterday when Felix's body had been retrieved from the bottom of
the mountain lake, but we heard about it only late last night.

'Thank you for coming,' the father said. His eye bags bulged.
'Please follow me upstairs.'

There were about twenty people inside the cramped living
room that also served as the kitchen and dining area. They all
stared at us the moment we entered the house. On the wall
hung a calendar-poster of God the Father, His long white beard

flowing down. He was surrounded by three cherubim in white whose bodies were chopped off from the necks down. All the heavenly figures floated on a dirty, yellow cloud.

After Mrs Santos had introduced herself, Felix's mother stood up. She was a large woman with a tired face. Her hair fell on her shoulders like tangled cobwebs. She walked over and gripped the hands of Mrs Santos.

And then she began to cry. Mrs Santos embraced her. In a voice like sandpaper, the mother said: 'I did not allow him to go out with his friends, Ma'am. He said they'd swim only in a shallow mountain lake in Boso-boso, five of them, their last excursion together before summer begins. Before they separate from each other. But I did *not* allow him . . .'

'I understand . . . I'm sorry,' was all Mrs Santos could say.

The mother continued: 'My son is gone, Ma'am. He has left us, he who is the brightest among my brood of ten, the eldest who promised to send his younger siblings to school, my dearest Felix. I'm only a laundrywoman, and my husband a carpenter but we would have done everything so he could finish college.'

The father turned away and looked out of the empty window.

Mrs Santos and I walked over to the coffin of Felix. Its texture was rough and it was painted dirty white, unlike the old worn pair of black shoes—with its lines like an old person's face—the shoes that Felix had scrupulously dyed and kept clean every day of the school year.

Sticks of tall yellow candles guttered and glowed around the coffin. I tried to pray, but instead, in my mind ran images of Felix: the Felix who laughed so loud one teacher told the class he was fit enough to be tied, and the Felix who sometimes stared into space, as if waiting for someone to come home. I would have also joined Felix and my other classmates that day on the lake, except that my mother asked me to accompany her to the department store.

An old woman, who must have been Felix's aunt, offered us a glass of soda and a plate of biscuits. As we ate, various voices floated in the thick, cramped air, merging with the heat-haze that only sharpened all the other smells in the slums.

The voices. They told of how Felix could not be found by his four young friends who had dove and scoured the very bottom of the lake several times over. Of how, in growing panic, the young friends ran and ran until they saw a clump of thatched huts and in broken voices told the people of the accident. Of how the mountain folk told them of the nymph who lives in the bottom of the mountain lake and takes the life of a young man every year, and so far, no bodies have surfaced from the depths of the lake. Of how the mountain folk rented a jeepney that took them to the mayor, who in turn contacted the Navy. Of how a Navy frogman in his webbed limbs dove into the lake of fifteen feet, thinking this would be an easy job, scouring the shallow depths of a landlocked body of water. But he surfaced again and again, shaking his head. Of how he dove again into the darkness of the lake, when he saw through his mask a diaphanous woman in white. Her head was bowed low, her long, black hair streaming down her face. When the diver sensed she had no face, he wanted to flee. But he stayed when he finally saw Felix, bloated beyond belief, lying near the feet of the woman. Of how the Navy frogman talked to the woman in his thoughts, begging her to please let go of the boy. He was reminded of his own son, who must be as young as this boy now lost in the lake. Of how the woman in white finally turned her back and was gone, swallowed up by the gloom of the lake. Of how the Navy frogman cradled the broken body, like father to son, then swam up, breaking the water's surface, finally back into the world of air and light. Of how the moment the bloated body was laid gently on a flat rock, the eardrums of Felix exploded. Of how the old women of the mountain shook their heads and clucked their tongues in both pity and fear. Of how the mortician in the town had much difficulty putting colour back on Felix's face, which had begun to assume the greyness of the lake on the mountain top.

* * *

W e were all fourteen years old, studying in the public high school beside the crumbling marketplace in Project 4. I studied there because the Salesian Brothers in Mandaluyong did not allow me to enrol in their school since classes had already begun, even if I carried a glowing letter of recommendation from the Father Principal of Don Bosco in Bacolor, a letter in long, flowing script, that began with the words, '*Shalom, Brother.*'

I studied in that high school and stayed there, while my mother taught music and my father worked in Saudi Arabia. There was a strange pleasure in growing up in the city, throbbing with its myriad joys: the huge department stores with their colourful shops of candies and toys and the live mannequins glassed-in on display windows in front of the stores, moving their arms and heads every five minutes or so; Fiesta Carnival with its endless rides and games; the cool, dark movie houses spinning their many tales of terror and love on the screen.

I was fourteen when I felt I was changing. No, not only the hair growing all over my body and the voice breaking again and again in the most embarrassing moments. I was trapped in my strange, dark moods. Even in the midst of family and friends, I would sometimes stop, gripped by a sadness so sudden yet so strong. I would still remember Luis, his face seared in my memory. At nights I would sometimes get my extra pillow and hug it tightly, wishing it were him whom I missed. Sometimes, I would just walk and walk, looking for a crack in the wall, wishing I could hide there forever.

Outside it was hostile. The president had just proclaimed himself concurrently as the prime minister, following the footsteps of his idol, Adolf Hitler. The First Lady fell on her knees at the Notre Dame in Paris, praying with her diamond rosary whose beads glistened like tears. And the church was telling me all my pleasures were forbidden. In his mosquito-infested confessional box at the Immaculate Heart of Mary Church, speaking in his odd English with a heavy Spanish accent, Fr Gabriel Garcia Marquez de Espadaña intoned his warning of brimstone and hellfire if I would continue reading pornography, thinking pornography, and doing pornography to myself. Would he curse me in three languages if I told him there was nothing else in the world I wanted except Roel Vergel de Dios, who had the face of an angel and the body of a Greek god?

My father in Saudi Arabia wrote interminable letters and sent me many voice tapes. He said it was so hot in Riyadh that his nose would often times bleed when the temperature shot past 100 degrees Fahrenheit. That he would just stay there for two years and come home immediately to start a business of his own. That he was surrounded by so many Filipinos—engineers and nurses and hairdressers and janitors—the babble of Tagalog could be heard competing with the calls of the muezzin, which were issued from the mosques five times a day. He always reminded me to shape up for the business management course I would take up in college. My mother wanted me to fold my blanket and fix my bed sheet every morning and never leave my dirty clothes lying around, like the flaked-off skin of a moulting snake. Together, they both told me to avoid parties, because 1) I would learn to smoke dope there, and the government's slogan of the season was *No Hope in Dope*; 2) my friends would tell me to have sex with my girlfriend (*my girlfriend?*), and what if I make her pregnant?; and 3) later, on the way home, I might meet with an accident (or be stabbed, or held up, times are truly dangerous).

My literature teacher, Miss Kring Kring Caticlan, wanted me to parrot her exact words, flunking me in the exams, or giving me her famous dagger look, when I disregarded the 'moral lessons' she always pinned on every poem and story we discussed, like butterflies pinned to the wall. Once, she asked us to report on a poem called 'Erotique'. Listen:

Lust is rearing up and neighing and kicks at the soul.
Freedom, freedom is all that it wants.
It rises, it rises on its hind legs when you rein it in.
O how difficult to master it even with a whiplash in hand.

I said in my report that the poem was about unbridled lust, which the persona compared to a horse (apt metaphor, that) but Miss Caticlan cut me short before I could finish my report. My teacher—who had a Master of Arts in Family Life and Child Development from the University of Gumamugam—insisted that the poem is simply about freedom. This, she added, her eyes as opaque as the eyes of dolls in horror films, is proven by two things: the first is by the use of the word 'freedom' that is even explicitly mentioned in the poem, and the second is the horse that she said is used in military battles.

I was fourteen when I decided to plug the crack in the wall: I fell in love with a beautiful girl named Melissa. I did not know how it happened, just the days clicking into place, her large, limpid eyes haunting me in my dreams. The shirtless Roel Vergel de Dios leaning on the branch of a tree seemed to have vanished in my mind and memory. Now there was a woman who would be my anchor, so I would never again wander. I followed her around on campus and inserted perfumed love letters between the pages of her biology textbook written by Dr Dolores Hernandez. I took a bath twice a day and brushed my teeth five times a day and put on my father's

Jovan musk perfume on the back of my ears, as *Teen Magazine* said I should do. I spent endless hours before the oval mirror in my parents' room, practising my smile, making sure I could flash that dazzling smile in the best angle imaginable the moment she passed by.

Life was air and water, earth and fire.

One day, after our biology class, I went to her and asked her if we could talk. 'Yes, on my way home,' she said, without smiling. Her lips were like a straight line. I knew then that the whole class knew that we would walk home together. I heard one of the boys say, 'Not really a faggot, I told you so,' while the girls giggled because they had all read my letters on the scented stationeries I used, passed from hand to hand during the afternoon break.

In the insane heat of March, I walked Melissa to her jeepney stop and told her I loved her. Just like that. 'I don't know why. You are beautiful and you are kind,' I said, looking down at the dusty ground.

She was quiet for a while. Then she said, 'You are very nice. You are good-looking and you're very bright.'

And then I knew it would come, the sudden blast on the face, the stormy weather in the heart that began with three letters. '*But* can we be just friends?'

Mayday, Mayday, I wanted to say, but Melissa had already patted my arm and taken a jeepney bound for Murphy.

The street had become a desert, and the sun seared me so. I went home in a daze. I saw my whole life crumble before me. At home, Ludy was cooking my favourite chicken *tinola,* the fragrance of crushed ginger and pepper leaves floating in the air. My mother was still in school. I went to my room, locked the door, and drew the grey curtains over the window. Then I rested my tired body on the bed. I tried to sleep but a tear seeped from my left eye, slipped down my cheek, then lodged itself in my ear. Soon, there was a torrent of tears, and in the violence of falling waters, I wished I would just sleep now and forever and never ever wake up.

But I did wake up, after two hours, my stomach growling with hunger, and then had a lovely dinner of hot chicken *tinola*, the pepper leaves and the ginger and the aroma of it all! In front of me hung the tapestry of *The Last Supper*, the colours deeper and darker than before. Jesus Christ was surrounded by his disciples: one like a rock, the other a traitor signalled by the crowing of a cock. I stood up, walked past the piano covered with a crocheted white top, past the photograph of my then-young father posing in front of his military dormitory on a wintry day at the Air Force Academy in Colorado Springs, his knee-high boots buried in the snow.

Then I took a long walk outside. No wind whistled among the leaves. And when I looked up there were no stars, just shards of glass scarring the sky . . .

For days on end, I tried to forget her. I faced the daily rigours of life as normally as possible. Graduation time came, and I was awarded the First Honours. My mother was filled with such joy that she bought me a pair of blue Dockers. My father sent me another watch, a Bulova. Melissa came and congratulated me. I just looked at her vacantly. I knew that I would always be sad. I was again missing Luis. Then, during one long night of wakefulness, I stood up from my bed, walked over to the half-opened window, and rested my forehead on the cold glass pane.

Outside, there was nothing, only a field of darkness and wind that was almost wet. Then it came to me, dimly at first, then later, in gathering whorls of light until it was fierce with clarity: the slippery image of the Navy frogman in the darkness of the lake, begging the nymph to let go of Felix.

She did let go, in the end.

For a long time after that, I thought that if the world had a skin, it would be broken and grey all over, like the body of Felix, who had died when we were all lost, and fourteen.

Yes, the Miss Universe

The Bank for International Reconstruction and Development (BIRD) based in Washington, D.C., held their XXth annual meeting in Manila.

'This historical event,' crowed the president that night on all the TV stations (which again zapped *Wonder Woman* off the screen, she who pilots an invisible plane) 'proves that the bankers of the world agree that we have indeed marshalled our resources very well and turned our history of defeat into a future of hope.'

From that point, a flurry of questions had to be answered. How to house the world's bankers in the luxury they had been accustomed to? Faster than Harry Houdini, the money from the Development and Aid Package of BIRD was diverted to the construction of seven new five-star hotels.

And so the commuters and office workers from Manila to Makati had to suffer monstrous traffic jams as one hotel rose after another in front of Manila Bay. One wag compounded the nightmare by suggesting that brick walls be erected between the city and the bay. The people protested that the walls would block their view of Manila's magnificent sunset. Others grumbled that the government only wanted to hide the people living in the slums, who had begun to build their shanties of rusty, corrugated-tin roof and soggy cardboard by the seawall. The truly wicked said, no, the government only wanted to raise more revenue by charging 100 pesos for anybody who wanted to see the sunset flaming barbarously beyond the wall.

Both hotels and walls were finished, along with a sprawling international convention centre that could rival anything found in Japan. What about the bankers' cars? Seven hundred late-model Mercedes Benzes were imported, and the citizens of Manila were treated to the sight of the Benzes gliding by, absorbing the shocks from the potholes and the uneven paving of the roads, their windows tinted evenly against the harsh tropical sun.

After the bankers came the beauty contest.
Margarita Mon Amour was chosen Miss Philippines the previous year. Many people thought the judges should have chosen somebody fairer, with a more aquiline nose, to represent the country in the Miss Universe contest held in Athens. They said Margarita won only because she graduated *magna cum laude* from an exclusive girls' school and had a grandfather who was a Justice in the Supreme Court.

But Margarita—with her wide forehead, her big and intelligent eyes, her full and sensuous lips—won in Athens. Even before the coronation night, the Greek press was already gushing about the 'dusky beauty from the Philippines who walked regally like a queen'. 'Like Helen,' another paper gushed, 'who could launch a thousand wars, errr, ships.' And so on coronation night itself, Margarita Mon Amour went to the Parthenon in a simple silk gown the colour of mother-of-pearl, her blue-black hair in a bun. She played a haunting *kundiman* on the bamboo nose flute, the audience stunned into silence by the sadness of the love song. She later went through the rigmarole of the Q and A with aplomb.

Bob Barker: 'Miss Philippines, what is the square root of 11,250 divided by 40 then multiplied by 99?'

Margarita Mon Amour: 'How much time do I have?'

A nd now she was here, walking on the stage of the Folk Arts Theatre, while the wind from the sea cooled the audience that had already crowded the First Lady's latest project. Manila being Manila—this mad, maternal city of our many myths and memories—everybody was jumping at the thought of the city hosting the Miss Universe contest that year. The machos were especially ecstatic, as day by day the tabloids splashed photos of their favourite candidates in skimpy bathing suits, getting their lovely tan from the glittering tropical sun.

So on this night of nights, the candidates flounced onstage, speaking in various tongues, a Babel of greetings that were beamed worldwide. Miss Brazil came in a dress whose colours could make the parakeets in her country blush. Miss United States of America came from Texas and wore the tightest cowgirl jeans Manila had ever seen. Miss Philippines was Guadalajara de Abanico, a *mestiza* who had the habit of turning her finely-chiselled nose up at every social function and who, Manila's reporters complained, always arrived late. 'I'm sure there's a friar somewhere in the family line,' snapped Istariray X., mother hen of Manila's society columnists, in her bitchy column called W.O.W. ('Woman of the World').

T he favourites of the Manila press included Miss Wales, Helen Morgan, because she had pendulous breasts; Miss Spain, Amparo Muñoz, the 20-year-old *señorita* from Barcelona who looked like the Blessed Virgin Mary; and Miss Finland, Johanna Raunio, because she looked like the girl in the Bear Brand milk commercial. The country exploded with joy when the three were called as finalists, along with Miss Aruba, Maureen Ava Viera, whom the Manila press called 'Black Beauty' even if she was brown, and the *señorita* from Colombia, Maria Ella Cecilia Escandon, who had the face of the Lord's handmaiden.

The judges please:

1. Gloria Diaz who won the Miss Universe in 1969, just when the Americans were landing on the moon. Like Margarita Mon Amour, she was not your typical Filipina beauty queen, for she was short, brown, sassy and smart. During her final Q and A, she was asked. 'If the first man on the moon suddenly materializes in front of your door, what would you tell him?' Quick as a gazelle, Gloria Diaz answered: 'Well, I will tell him what I would tell any other man who would come calling on me. Please come in and would you like to have some snacks? I am sure he would be ravenous, eating as he did only pills and tablets while in outer space.' Thunderous applause. After she won, she was asked if she had a message for the three American astronauts. She said: 'Well, the United States has conquered the moon, but the Philippines has conquered the universe.'

2. Zenaida Carajo, also called Baby, who smiled through her tenth facelift and had difficulty walking, because on her neck, arms and fingers glittered the country's second-heaviest diamonds (after the First Lady's). She also wore makeup so thick that people called her Kabuki Lady behind her back. Or even *espasol*, the dessert from the south smothered in layer upon layer of flour.

3. Joseph Carajo, Baby's cousin, who taxed the country's seven million farmers with a levy ostensibly to fund the planting of mahogany trees to produce 'modern antique furniture', but the funds were allegedly hidden in places as far as the British Virgin Islands.

4. Richard Head, the American Ambassador, called Dick by two camps: the grim-and-determined Marxists and the applicants denied visas by His Honour's consuls.

5. Bernardo Tulingan, who called himself the country's finest painter, with his grotesqueries hanging like chopping boards in Manila's seafood restaurants.

6. Zosimo Zaymo, a successful talent manager famous for pimping his female models in Brunei and fondling the male ones before hidden cameras.

7. The young Emmanuel, bright and beady-eyed opinion columnist par excellence, thinking how soon he could sleep with as many contestants as possible.

8. Mother China, the country's number-one movie producer, who loved to have zombies in her movies.

9. And, of course, the First Lady herself, the chair of the board of judges, Her Majesty Infinitely Brighter than the Blaze of Ten Thousand Suns.

One by one the winners were called, to deafening applause: Miss Aruba, fourth runner-up; Miss Colombia, third runner-up; Miss Finland, second runner-up. And then, only Miss Wales and Spain were left. Both held hands and braced themselves for the announcement, their eyes closed, chins quivering.

The Blessed Virgin Mary lookalike, of course, won. After she was called as the newest Miss Universe, Amparo Muñoz gave the crowd a beatific smile, tears running down her face, ruining her makeup. But never mind, for here was Margarita Mon Amour, gliding on the stage, relinquishing cape, crown and sceptre, and then the señorita walked around the stage, the flashbulbs popping forever.

Miss Universe would constantly visit Manila as part of the First Lady's entourage of royalty and celebrities, who would be flown to the city to inaugurate a massive new building (part of what critics called the First Lady's Edifice Complex), or just have a party aboard the presidential yacht, *RPS Ang Pangulo,* on Manila Bay. Later, Amparo Muñoz would star in porn movies in her country, precious copies of which were smuggled into Manila and shown at the parties of the rich and the brain-dead, for they married within the family to keep their fabulous, feudal wealth intact.

Helen Morgan would play the lead role in a Filipino film called *Nagalit ang Umaga Dahil sa Sobrang Haba ng Gabi (The Morning Got Mad Because the Night was Too Long)*, where she bared her breasts, then returned to her cold, grey island after the film did dismally at the tills.

Johanna Raunio joined the Miss International contest in Tokyo and won. Ella Cecilia Escandon became a writer of Latin American telenovelas, the most popular of which—*Mari Mar, Ay!*—was shown in an obscure Philippine station, promptly became number one, and wiped the smug grins off the faces of the smart suits running the number-one network. And Maureen Ava Viera married a wealthy Filipino, divorced him, then returned to the Caribbean, to run as governor of Aruba. She won by a majority of the votes.

News Item: A Surprise for Miss Nicaragua

During the Parade of Beauties of the Miss Universe contestants on Roxas Boulevard, one man jumped aboard the float of Miss Nicaragua, Mildred de Ortega, and hugged her tightly. Filipino security agents, quick as ever, were already dragging the man away 'for routine investigation', when the Miss Universe contestant, who was then already in tears, said, 'No, no, please, *por favor.*'

It turned out the man, who was a mestizo, was the brother of Miss Nicaragua herself. Danilo de Ortega had been in exile in the United States for five years, when that country was not yet being run by the Man with the Orange Hair. 'I was glad to know my sister has been chosen Miss Nicaragua. I used my savings as a waiter in Los Angeles so I could fly to Manila just to see her. I miss her and my family.'

Why did Danilo flee his country?

Perhaps it must have been the series of terrible earthquakes that tore his country apart, forcing Danilo to emigrate from his beautiful and peaceful country, opined Juan Tabaco, a highly paid columnist and a friend of the President. During a dinner party, said the clandestine Opposition press, a member of the Opposition—with much help from Johnny Walker Black—stood before Señor Tabaco and began to sing a song that I used to hear on the radio: *How much is that puppy in the window, arf arf.* And the eyes of Señor Tabaco—who used to write third-rate novels before the dictatorship co-opted him—began to fill with bitter tears.

When he was interviewed, Danilo Ortega simply said, 'I cannot stand the military dictatorship in my country.'

The mainstream press simply ignored that comment.

Poinsettias

Under the pine trees, three girls were walking to the Session Hall in Teachers' Camp, their light-brown uniforms blending with the softly falling dusk in the mountain city of Baguio.

I slung my blue jacket on my shoulders and stood up from the stone steps of Benitez Hall. My classmates had gone ahead of me. The sun was beginning to dip behind the trees, leaving a wash of colours—pink and salmon and red, with tints of grey that deepened with the night.

The emcee was a short young man with hair slicked to one side. He introduced the director of the 20th Quezon City High School Senior's Conference, a big, muscled man with a voice that matched his build. The emcee also called onstage the coordinators for accommodations, meals, security, secretariat and socials. Polite applause. From where I sat at the back, the newsletter coordinator was a plain-looking girl, tall and skinny. The coordinators were last year's students; this year, they volunteered to help run the conference.

The French windows in the newsletter room were wide open. A chill wind roamed inside. I buttoned my jacket and turned up its collar.

'Hi!' called out a voice that was warm and even. I turned around. The newsletter coordinator. She was nearly as tall as I, her head tilted regally to one side. She had a big mouth and bee-stung lips. She looked like a model.

'Hello,' I said. 'I'm Danny Cruz, and you're the newsletter editor, right?'

'Yes, I'm Roxanne, Roxanne Gonzales.' She had high cheekbones and a wide forehead. Her jaws were angular, the kind of face you'd see on a magazine cover. She looked like Margarita Mon Amour, Miss Universe of 1974. Her eyes were large and they had a way of turning brown in the light. But when she smiled, I thought I saw sadness in those eyes.

'Please fill in the personal data sheet. We'll wait for the others to arrive.' She turned around and walked to the door, pasting a piece of paper scrawled with 'NEWSLETTER' in blue pentel pen on the door. Her shiny hair flowed down her shoulders. Black Levi's hugged her long, long legs.

Roxanne presided over the meeting. 'Jhun-jhun, Let-let, and Mai-mai, please interview the delegates for the *Gazette* issue. Ask them about the trip from Manila. First impressions, fresh impressions.'

'What about me, Roxanne?' said the guy across from me. He looked like an airhead, one of those guys who had nothing between his ears, except earwax. His name was Jonathan Livingstone Sy Go.

'Okay, Jon. Can you write an editorial based on the theme of the conference? The theme is . . .'

'Oh, yes, I know: "Youth: Moral Values in the New Decade."'

'Oh, nice to know *you* know the theme. Now write an editorial, please, around 250 words, okay, Jon?' Beneath the cool voice, I noticed a quick temper. And then she looked at me.

'Danny, could you please do the literary page?'

'Okay. Will do.' Then I smiled to catch her attention.

She ignored me, then she added. 'Please turn in all assignments by 5 p.m. If there are no more questions, you may go to your rooms and rest. There's an acquaintance party tonight. Enjoy.'

Everybody stood up and left the room, except me.

'Aren't you going to the party?'

'No, I've two left feet, you know. How about you?'

A sigh. Then: 'I've to finish this for a paper in class.' She showed me a small book bound in black cloth. *A Farewell to Arms.* 'Don't let me keep you here,' she said.

Oh, you only want to continue reading the love story of Catherine and Lieutenant Henry, I wanted to tease her, but all I said was goodbye.

Inside my room, I took off my jeans and changed into the blue Nike jogging pants my father gave me last Christmas. I lit a cigarette, a habit I began only last month. Like many of my classmates, the first time I smoked I did it in the bathroom of our house. It must be those adverts (*Come to Marlboro country*), with the cute and hairy cowboy in the tough brown leather jacket and black boots because I had a hard-on the first time I smoked in the bathroom of our house.

The cigarette butt glowed. Smoke quivered in the air. I wanted to be alone, to think, because I was confused again. I heard the wind, a sound lost instantly amongst the pine trees. I thought I heard a familiar voice, floating from another country. I stood up and closed the windows. What shall I give the *Gazette*? A poem, perhaps?

I picked up my pen and yellow pad paper. Writing. Writing was like a sudden urge, an itch, a kind of lust even. The words ran inside me, like blood.

* * *

In Bulacan, I saw farmers in threadbare pants and faded shirts. Behind them lay the fields heavy with ripe grains. When we reached

Pampanga, a mountain broke the smoothness of the horizon. Mount Arayat. The familiar mountain of memory. Above it, the sky was an immense blueness.

We stopped for lunch at the Vineyard, a restaurant in Rosales, Pangasinan. After lunch and pissing in one of those toilets where you held your breath so you would not have a migraine later, we went back to our buses. We passed a bridge with steel girders and high arches. But below it lay burning sand and stones, not the mighty, roaring river I had expected.

When the air became raw and sharp, I knew we were going up Kennon Road. Suddenly, smoke came from the hood of the La Mallorca. 'The bus is burning!' cried the girl behind me.

The driver stood up, a stocky man with a beer belly and skin the colour of dry earth. 'We only need water. Don't worry, we'll be all right,' he said. My teacher, Mrs Genova, noisily volunteered her Tupperware filled with water. We snickered.

Then we continued with the trip. Mountain and sky, river and ravine. The sight of a landslide made us shift in our seats again. It was a four-month-old landslide, caused by Typhoon Miling. One side of the mountain was gone but the landslide had created a wide and calm lake. From the lake, a young tree was beginning to grow.

And when we reached Baguio, the first things I saw were the poinsettias, like splashes of blood on the face of a hill. My biology textbook said the red petals of the poinsettias were not really flowers, but leaves.

Thus, you can say that the poinsettias are masters of disguise.

* * *

I would have awakened later but for the noise in the room. 'That Ruby from Holy Family Academy has a very soft body,' said Bing Bong.

I plumped my pillow into a fat missile and aimed it at him.

'You're just jealous. Where did you go last night?' asked Bing Bong.

Mario was my new classmate. He was wearing only his undershirt and his shorts, showing his young, hard biceps and hairy thighs. I always looked at him surreptitiously in our physical education class, when he would be wearing his abbreviated shorts and sleeveless grey shirt. When I met Mario, Luis's face began to get hazy in my mind.

And now Mario said, 'I saw him in the newsletter room. Seems like he's making a pass at the newsletter coordinator. Remember the *Vogue* model?'

I wanted to say, 'You're just jealous, Mario,' but I held my horses. I found Mario cute, and he always teased me. He must have sensed that I liked him, even if I did not show it directly, which was my wont. I said, 'Hey, I wasn't making a pass at her.' Then: 'But of course, I'd love to . . .'

Mario just smiled at me, a wicked glint in his eyes.

After breakfast, we went to the Session Hall. The list of delegates and the groups they belonged to were tacked on the bulletin board. I belonged to Group 5, with my classmates Edgar Allan Pe and Daffodil Tulip Pastilan. During the first session, Daffodil was elected secretary and I, chairman. In the afternoon, Attorney Honey Boy Velez in a dark-blue suit bored us to death when he gave a two-hour speech on the theme of the conference that began with national hero Jose Rizal's quote, 'The youth is the hope of the Fatherland.' *Lolo* Pepe must be break-dancing in his grave by now. I sat at the back and doodled.

After the sessions ended, I left my essay in the newsletter room, with a short note for Roxanne. After dinner of fresh vegetables and sweet-and-sour fish *escabeche*, I walked back to the room and saw her, but she was busy reading Hemingway. On the table lay my essay, unread.

I rushed back to my room, hands deep in the pockets of my jacket, gnats of annoyance following me. My classmates were all there. Mario said we should drink. We pooled our money, then sent Nick, Gerry and Mandy to smuggle a case of beer. We tried to be quiet since drinking was against the house rules but as the empty beer bottles multiplied, the noise level also rose. My classmates told stories and jokes about women with boobs like the bumper of a car, or what they would do if they met Bo Derek on the beach. We smoked and drank and burped. A haze began to form before me, followed by a hiss of words: *'I like you, but I'm sorry . . .'* Sheena had said that evening in their yard, the garden perfumed with *ylang-ylang* and jasmine. *'My family is moving to Canada in summer. Let us write to each other. Good luck and best wishes . . .'* The beer bubbled and foamed, and I drank my San Miguel cold and bitter. So many departures and few arrivals . . . Afterward, I was so drunk I just staggered to my bed and fell asleep. *Good luck and best wishes.* As if she were congratulating a mere acquaintance on her graduation day. Sheena and I had been dating for a year. We would watch films at Virra Mall and fumble with each other's clothes in the dark. But being convent-bred she had her rules. The navel was the border zone. Everything below that was a no-no. So while watching *Blue Lagoon* I would French kiss her and run my tongue around her nipples and try to pull down her Bang Bang Jeans, but she always slapped my hand. The noise of a hand being slapped would bring snickers from the other lovers around us. We would stop and look at each other, and then begin kissing again. I whispered to my Catholic girlfriend that the pillar of salt wanted to see the burning bush, but she would not hear of it. She would just kiss me back and embrace me tightly, running her fingers down my spine. I always went home with a bad case of blue balls. Those were truly, ah, painful moments.

The sunlight streaming from the window woke me up. I got up from bed with a hard-on. My classmates were still asleep. All bombed out. Mario slept on the bed next to mine. His grey, woollen blanket had already fallen on the floor. He was wearing his white jockeys. He also had a hard-on, which tent-poled his jockeys. I had to tear myself away from the Tower of Babel so I could start my morning.

I went to the bathroom and took a shower. I washed and lathered my face, and then I shaved. I remembered my dream last night (Mario and I taking a bath together, at dawn, our fingers exploring each other's bodies), and I slapped cold water on my face. These hormones were so confusing. I had to pull myself together because later in the day would be the panel interview for the Ten Most Outstanding Delegates of the conference.

The director, the conference secretary, and a man introduced as the dean of an Opus Dei university interviewed us. The results would be added to the scores each candidate got for their performance during the conference. We were interviewed individually, behind closed doors. It was all beginning to sound like the Miss Universe beauty contest, and so while they interviewed me, I sat straight, with my right foot pointed forward.

The first two questions were a breeze. The Opus Dei dean, who looked like any of your kind uncles, asked the third question: 'What do you think of such adolescent preoccupation as smoking, drinking, and drugs?' He spat the word *adolescent* from his lips as if it were some illness.

I was uneasy because I had expected a question about the conference itself. He was sooooo damned smug I said, 'Well, sir, I think drinking is not so bad especially if done in a social gathering. Smoking you can do if you want to have yellow, nicotine-stained fingernails. Drugs, I would like to believe, would be too expensive.'

'So do you smoke, or drink or take drugs?' he said, taking off his thick glasses that looked like goggles, and then fixed his sharp eyes on me.

What the hell do you care? I wanted to tell him, but I kept my cool. He who blows his top first, loses. 'Of course, as I said, I would drink socially, which means when my peers pressure me. I smoked for a while, but the nicotine stained my fingernails and teeth and so I stopped. Drugs? I don't know where to find them, maybe you have an idea where?' I would have rambled on, but the dean had told me to stop.

During the awarding ceremonies, after the emcee had called the names of the tenth down to the second most outstanding delegate, I knew I had lost. I was sitting beside Mario, inhaling the fragrance of his *Brut*. The night was cold and our warm thighs were grazing each other. I was thinking of the many things I could do to his hairy thighs when my name was called as the most outstanding delegate. Mario gripped my hand tightly, and then he hugged me. I wished he would never let go. But he did, and so I walked to the stage and received my heavy gold medallion and a certificate done in sheepskin. My classmates' Instamatic cameras kept on popping.

The Opus Dei vote could only pull me down a few points, I heard later from the grapevine that always clung and grew after the results of any contest had been announced. After the awarding ceremonies, there were some more boring speeches so I asked Mario, 'Would you like to take a walk? It's cooler outside.'

Down the footpath we walked. Dusk had already settled amongst the leaves, and the air was heavy with the clean fragrance of pine. A moon hung in the sky, ripe and full and yellow, like a harvest moon. Is there still a man on the moon? I wondered suddenly, remembering Ludy's tale one childhood night so many years ago. But I let the memory go.

Mario and I sat on a concrete bench encircling a dry fountain. A mermaid in stone sat in the centre of the fountain.

'Congratulations again,' Mario said, as he sat beside me. Vapour rose from his lips as he spoke.

'Thank you,' I answered. He looked good in his black long-sleeved denim shirt, with one button down, and black jeans. His eyes were big and penetrating. I wanted so much to touch his face and tell him I liked him. I knew he knew what I wanted to tell him, but the words remained frozen on my tongue.

It was he who broke the awkward silence. 'Perhaps we should be heading back?' Then he snickered. 'I think any moment now a snowflake would settle on the tip of my nose.'

Which I would melt with a kiss, I wanted to say, dangerously witty to the very end. But all I could say was 'Yes, you're right'. Then I swallowed, down my gut, all the words I wanted him to hear, every single one of them. Suddenly, the brightest young person in this gathering was struck dumb. Like gold medallions to the thumb.

We walked back to the hall, the heavy darkness and mist smothering us. We sat down and tried to make small talk amidst all that noise. I knew then that he had already let me go. I was crushed, but being an Aries I never showed my defeat. Early on in life I have learnt that you could always sheathe everything with irony and wit.

The farewell party went on. The DJ played that stupid song about Wolfgang Amadeus Mozart. But when he played 'Morning Girl', Mario suddenly stood up. He walked clear across the darkened hall, to a girl in a pink frothy dress. Barbie smiled and stood up and walked with him to the centre of the dance floor. His arms tightened about her waist and they danced so close to each other. For once, I wished the dean from the Opus Dei were here, to tell Mario that there should be distance between him and his doll, 'so your respective guardian angels could pass by'.

I wanted to laugh, but I was afraid my face would just crack from all the sadness inside me. Quietly I slipped out of the room, ignoring everybody who was congratulating me. All along, my gold medallion as the Most Outstanding Delegate hung in my chest. I only forced a smile when I saw Roxanne, who was asking me if I had seen my essay published in the last issue of the *Gazette*. I just nodded, and walked away. I was walking into a door, another door, an infinity of doors.

Down the stairs I ran until I reached the dark yard. My arm brushed against the poinsettias hanging like bouquets in the empty air. But when I turned to look at them, small beads of water were glittering on the red leaves.

YSL

'Laurent, Yves Saint,' said the Manila paper tacked on the board.

I was enrolling for college at Saint Ignatius University and in front of me was a big version of the registration form I had to fill in. 'Laurent' (surname), 'Yves' (first name), 'Saint' (middle name). I wanted to correct the entries and put 'Saint' as part of the surname, but what the heck! Five hundred freshmen were enrolling, so what was the problem with a snooty example?

I had been lucky with official letters, so far. After graduating valedictorian from high school (but feigning tonsillitis so I could skip the junior-senior prom), I had been receiving letters.

The State University said I could take Business Administration and Accounting in Diliman. My father recommended this course to me, since he said it would make me rich.

Then Saint Ignatius University said I could take English Literature in Loyola Heights, but only on a partial scholarship since my father was working overseas and I was an only child. My mother smirked. 'But we have a thousand relatives knocking on our door, and the inflation rate has been rising like anything!'

And the third letter solved everything for me. It came from the director of the Bureau of Posts, no less. He said I had won the first prize in the Association of Southeast Asian Nations (ASEAN) Essay-writing Contest for high-school students. My prize: 5,000 pesos, five albums of ASEAN stamps, and a four-year scholarship to a university of my choice. A monthly stipend of 1,000 pesos and a book allowance of 2,000 pesos per semester sweetened the deal.

And that was how I became classmates with the sons and daughters of landowners and owners of factories, corporate lawyers and government ministers, generals and movie stars, ex-priests and tycoons. There were so many good-looking boys but I found them too fair, too flabby, too loose-limbed. There were so many good-looking girls but they chattered in a language only they could understand. *Syet, the ulan is about to fall na!*

Later, of course, the stereotypes all came tumbling down, like a pack of cards in *Alice in Wonderland*, and some of these rich brats even became my dearest friends.

The Heart of Summer

On the first day of April, we moved to a row house in a subdivision carved out of the Antipolo hills. A row house is a euphemism for the houses that somehow managed to fit into 120-square-metre lots. They looked like matchboxes, really, built near the riverbank. The larger houses, of course, stood grandly at the centre of the village, in front of the chapel. We would be renting the house from the mayor's mistress, one of three houses she owned there.

The living room of the house spilt over into the kitchen. The house only had two tiny rooms, but it was enough for us. The owner of the apartment we had been renting in Project 4 wrote to us (in pink stationery with the letterhead 'Dr Antonina Raquiza, PhD') to say that she would raise the monthly rent to five thousand pesos. If we could not agree to her new terms, we would have two months to vacate the apartment. Mama glared at the letter, then said something obscene about our landlady's father. A day later, she began poring over the adverts, looking for cheaper rent in the suburbs. Papa's monthly remittances from his engineer's job in Saudi would not be enough if the landlady raised the rent, since he was also sending some nephews and nieces to school. *Noblesse oblige* is how you call it, but it was actually more *oblige* than *noblesse*. And that was how we moved to Antipolo.

It was a long, hot summer. The days were dull and endless, a desert that stretched into infinity. During the afternoons, the heat fell on your skin like a whip. The water in the village water tank began drying up a week after we moved in, so Ludy and I had to fetch water from the fire hydrant in the street corner. Even though I hated studying in summer, this time, I actually looked forward to the first day of summer classes at the university.

But since Ludy also went home to Albay that summer (to look for a boyfriend and dance in the *baile*), I did the chores myself. Mama left the house every day for her piano tutorials. I did the laundry and fixed lunch. In the afternoons, I gathered the laundry so easily dried by the oppressive heat up here in the hills. I folded the clothes, then sorted them while watching the old Nida Blanca and Nestor de Villa *cha-cha-chas* on TV. Sometimes, I would read the short stories of Estrella Alfon (*Ay, Magnificence!*), or sketch faces and places on my drawing pad.

Then in the blue hour before dusk, I would pick up our red plastic pail and walk five houses away to the street corner to fetch water.

I would join the queue in the street corner. In front of me stood wooden carts full of drums, pails, and recycled gasoline containers. I carried only a pail but I was too timid to elbow my way to the head of the line. The short, stocky men nudged each other's ribs and exchanged stories: '*Pare*, Vodka Banana did it again in her latest penetration movie, *Only a Wall Between Us*.' The women gossiped about their movie idols: 'Sharon's legs are like a washerwoman's paddle,' said one, whose varicose veins strained on her legs like netting.

After a long wait, I finally reached the fire hydrant. From its open mouth gushed water whose pressure was so strong that it swirled round and round my pail, the foam then spilling on the dry earth. Afterward, I walked back to the house where I carefully poured the water into the drum. Then back to the street corner, again.

On my way back, darkness had already settled on the hills. The chickens would be roosting on the branches of the star-apple trees, and the cicadas would begin their eternal buzzing. When I reached the street corner again, a young man was standing at the head of the line. He was not there when I left earlier. He must have asked his housemaid to stand in for him, and returned only when it was time to fill his drum.

Dusk slept on his rumpled hair. Smooth, nut-brown skin. Eyes round as marbles. He wore a maroon T-shirt silk-screened with Mapua College of Engineering. Black jeans on long legs, then brown leather sandals.

When he saw me at the end of the line, he walked to me and said: 'Uy, *pare*, you can go ahead, since you only have this pail.' Cool, deep voice. 'Thank you,' I said. Then I smiled at him and followed him to the fire hydrant. I kept on looking surreptitiously at his hairy legs. When he looked at me, I would shift my attention to the water beginning to fill my pail, swirling round and round, until it flowed over the lips of the pail. I thanked him again, and then gave him my name. He mumbled his name. I smiled, and then walked away. I walked away because I was afraid that any moment now, I would tell Mark that I liked him not only because he was considerate but also because he had such well-muscled legs and clean toenails.

That summer, the Bermuda grass in our lawn had turned brown. We had hoped for a friendly neighbourhood, similar to the one we had left behind in Project 4, but we were disappointed. A young childless couple lived in the house on the left: both were working, holding down two jobs each like everybody else. We only saw them at Sunday Mass. On the right lived an elderly couple with an only child, a teenage daughter named Maribel, who liked to bike around the village in midriff shirts and very abbreviated shorts. Her father was a big man with the face of a bulldog, his voice booming across the yard when he barked, errr, spoke.

The minibus station in Cubao slouched on the street right after Epifanio de los Santos Avenue, the nerve centre of the metropolis. It was housed in a big, abandoned garage. On the hard, earthen floor, the spilt oil looked like lost, black continents on a map.

That summer, I enrolled in two courses: Business Statistics and Financial Accounting. I took up Business Management at Saint Ignatius University although the only thing I wanted to do in the world was to draw. Pencil to paper, lines slowly, inevitably, forming faces. Or watercolour to paper, letting the paper soak up the rainbow of colours, forming a wash of skies and oceans, infinities of blue.

But I had to go to Business School. And so I left the house at one o'clock in the afternoon, after lunch, preferring to take the minibus rather than risk my life in those jeepneys whose drivers think they were Mad Max. More mad than Max, actually.

During the first week of classes, I was still adjusting to the hassle of commuting from house to school to house again. It was much easier in Project 4. I would just hop aboard any Cubao-bound bus, get off behind Queen's Supermarket, and then walk all the way home.

Here, I would have to wait for the minibus to fill up with passengers before we could leave. The street would be choked with hawkers selling everything: freshly sliced vegetables that could be cooked with shrimp paste, big apples from New Zealand, jeans with fake brand names sewn on the back, tabloids with their headlines in red ink blown up to 72 points Times Roman ('Boa

Constrictor in Dept. Store/ Dressing Room Swallows/ Up Female Customers'). Big speakers would boom with songs from Guns N' Roses alternating with Air Supply. Food stalls offered everything, from cow's entrails floating in lemon-spiked congee to day-old chicks smothered in orange flour, then fried to a crisp. And in the air, a cumulus of black exhaust fumes while the president, his family and cronies bled the country dry. Him with his decrees that passed for the laws of the land; her, with her New York buildings and Picasso paintings. And then altogether now, the conjugal dictatorship parcelling the country between themselves. Shady deals were drawn for resources in the air (contracts to buy military helicopters), land (farms turned to high-end resorts) and water (lakes turned into private fish pens latticed with bamboo fences).

Oh, how I wish I could just flee from all of this. There is nothing here, really, in this city and in this country except a big, black hole that sucked you in and drowned you in its ooze of oil. I wish I could go away, but to where? To forestall what W.H. Auden called thoughts of 'elsewhereishness', I just fixed my eyes on my textbook, even if I could not read by the faint light of the minibus. I was doing this one night when I raised my face just as Mark was coming in. His white shirt was tucked in his baggy jeans. His shirt revealed the curve of his chest. He carried a T-square in one hand and two thick books in the other. His wide forehead was furrowed. He must have had a bad day, I thought, moving to the right side of my seat so I could see him better. I wanted him to sit beside me, I wanted to feel the warmth of his hand and thigh against mine, I wanted so much to ease his discomfort. But a man with halitosis sat beside me instead.

The driver finally came. The engine sputtered and roared, then crawled slowly out of the narrow street. Near the street corner, the air became smokier, loud with the cries of hawkers vending barbecued chicken's blood, barbecued chicken's entrails (IUD), barbecued chicken's feet (Adidas), and barbecued chicken's head (Helmet).

The shrill sound of a policeman's whistle rose above the vendor's cries. At the whistle's cry, the hawkers picked up their wares and then scattered madly in all directions. The charcoal embers left behind glowed eerily in the dark.

I was sitting in our front yard, admiring my mother's orchids, whose saplings she had asked from friends and which she had nurtured with uncommon care, now fully grown, the leaves shiny, with the texture of skin, and the flowers mottled with magenta and amber, the petals opening themselves layer upon layer to the dying afternoon sun.

As the petals opened, I felt myself entering a forest of limbs. Hair like seaweeds embraced those limbs. The thighs of the men were smooth like river stones. The V-shapes of their bodies glistened with sweat. Leaves like eyes covered their crotches. Under these leaves lay beautiful and breathing things.

I bolted upright with a start. I looked at the clock. The luminous hands pointed to almost midnight. My back was beaded with sweat, and in the room there was only unbearable heat. I remained motionless for a while, as my dream slipped away, and I was alone, again.

I stepped out of the room and headed for the kitchen. I turned the light on and made myself a cup of rice coffee—toasted rice turned into coffee. It was cheap and good for the heart. This was the coffee my mother and grandmother made in the forest during the dark days of the Japanese regime.

Cup in hand, I opened the front door. My skin brushed against the dry, brittle air. I sat down on the cemented stairs. To my left, the skeletal branches of the neighbour's *alibangbang* tree cut the moon into so many fragments.

I first smelt rather than heard the coming of the rain. The sound seemed to come from so far away. It was like a voice calling my name. The sound grew louder and louder by the second. I left the cup on the stair landing, stood up, and then ran barefoot in the yard. The whole house, the whole yard, the whole village seemed to be tense, waiting.

And then it came, puncturing holes in the night sky, rattling on the roofs, soaking wet both flowers and leaves: *Agua deMayo*! the first rains of May!

In the darkness, the rain's fingers caressed my hair and my face. It began licking my eyelids, my earlobes and my lips. I opened my mouth and let the rain's tongue roam inside me, while its fingers travelled downward, on my inner arm and on my chest. Its lips went around my nipples and navel, touching my warm, innermost spaces.

Like sunlight, heat rose from the earth, musky heat that entered my soles, warmed my body, and then broke out of the pores of my skin. It was brief but it pierced me beautifully, suddenly.

I knew now what I would do. I would soap myself in the bathroom, rinse my skin clean, change into fresh clothes that smell good and are crisp to touch. Then I would look for my sheets of Oslo paper in my drawer. I would run my fingers on my sketches of Mark. The rumpled hair and the dark, melancholy eyes. How could I tell him that there is nothing else in the world that I want than to be with him? Ludy said Mark would soon join his mother, who was working as a nurse in New York City. Many departures, few arrivals. But now, I have him: he is here, contained in the purity of my ache.

I would turn the lights off, plunging the house in darkness. Then I would turn myself over to the arms of sleep. Outside, the leaves would still be moist and breathing.

City Lights

Anna clasped her hands on the smooth Formica tabletop, raised her face, and said: 'I want to kill myself.'

Anna stood at four feet and ten inches tall, and she had the fragile air of a baby. She was a humanities major who vowed to write the Great Filipino Children's Story. Nothing reminded me of Anna's Spanish blood, except her mercurial temper: When it exploded, it sent sparks in the air, like the sharp movements of a flamenco dancer.

And now, she wanted to kill herself. I smoked on, unbelieving. A long line of students stretched before the greasy food counter of the university's cafeteria. Others sat and tittered with their after-lunch gossip. The voices fell over us, like a net.

'So, you've finally joined them?'

'Who's them?'

After clearing my throat, I answered: 'Those *artistes* suddenly filled with angst after reading Sylvia Plath. Do not forget the '*e*' in artiste.' I knocked my cigarette ashes on to the tray. 'Or Anne Sexton . . .'

'I'm sorry, but I don't belong there'. Her face flamed.

'All right, I'm sorry, Anna.'

The blades of the electric fan sliced through the haze of smoke and steam.

'I . . .' she began again, 'I want to tell you something.'

'Here?'

'Later. I've class at 2.30. Psych 21.'

'I'll hitch with you then?'

'Didn't bring the car.'

'Let's take public, okay?'

'Okay. See you then.'

*P*are, do you drink?' my classmate, Chito, asked me as we were walking down the stairs of Bellarmine Building. He was wearing moccasins the colour of old mahogany. We had just finished our quiz on the pre-revolutionary Filipino writers in Spanish.

'*Un poco,*' I answered, pleased with myself.

He smiled. I wished I had a face like that—clear, smooth skin; moustache carefully trimmed; lips like two delicate half-moons. That, and a lean yet muscular body, too. But Chito was just a friend; he never turned me on. '*Quieres a beber?*' He asked me if I wanted to drink.

'*Si, señor.* Okay, after that, no more,' I said, raising my hands. 'I'm running out of textbook phrases. Where?'

'Where else but the *Blue Box*?'

'Okay.'

The bulbs on the ceiling seemed to ripen as the night wore on. The art-deco lamp threw shadows on the soft bones of Chito's face. His hair was black waves tumbling down his head. He drank *San Miguel Beer* as if there were no classes the morning after, or as if he were drowning something, his bitten fingernails gripping each frosted bottle. All the while, he droned on and on about the war movies he had seen since he was a kid, *Papillon* and *Platoon* and *Apocalypse Now*, and the movies of Sylvester Stallone and Arnold Schwarzenegger. I kept up with his talk although I was beginning to get bored. Instead, I wanted to tell him why Barbara Streisand could only be photographed from one angle, or why Roberta

Flack's 'The First Time Ever I Saw Your Face' makes me weep, or why I would always love John Lennon (the mind, that quirky mind!), but would my macho friend even give me the time of day?

He insisted on paying, although I had suggested we split the bill. 'It's on me. I invited you out—and I drank twice as fast as you did.' He groped for his Calvin Klein wallet, called the waiter, and handed him a crisp five hundred-peso bill. After the waiter had gone, Chito showed me a picture of Minnie, his girlfriend. Of Chinese-Spanish-Filipino blood, Minnie had eyes that seemed to glow from a light inside her.

After dropping me off at the corner of Aurora and Katipunan, Chito's blue BMW zoomed away, leaving grains of dust in its wake.

Now, Anna and I were standing in the same corner, waiting for a jeepney that would take us to Cubao. From there, she would take a cab to Blue Ridge. It seemed she really wanted company, for she could have taken a cab direct to Blue Ridge but did not. I wanted to visit the bookstore in Cubao before going back to our apartment in Project 4.

I hailed a new jeepney whose miniature stainless-steel horses galloped on top of the hood. Inside, a flood of psychedelic lights. The B-52's 'There's a Moon in the Sky (Called the Moon)' bombarded us while we entered the jeepney. We picked our way through a forest of knees. We sat behind the driver. Around his neck coiled a Good Morning towel that used to be white.

Anna whispered: 'I want to tell you something.'

'Here?'

'Yes. I—I don't know why I should tell you this, but I've to get this out of me.'

I waited. On the jeepney's dashboard, a portrait of the Blessed Virgin Mary, with a garland of fresh jasmine buds. Beside her, a decal of a woman whose overripe body spilt out of her bikini. Some things would never change.

I waited. Then Anna whispered, 'I had my baby aborted. Four years ago.'

I was silent, trying to grope for the pack of *Marlboro* in my pocket.

'I'm not making it up,' she said in a soft, painful voice.

'Why?' I knew it was a dumb question, but I had to speak: My throat was turning dry.

Silence.

But when she spoke again, the words flowed on and on. 'I fell in love with Edwin, who was already married. I was only 16 years old. But you have met my mother, who runs our big family corporation like a military academy, she found out . . . I fought to keep the baby. But Papa—he hit me. Many times. They forced me to . . .'

Anna's fingernails dug into my arm.

'They forced me, and now, I'm afraid I won't be able to bear a child again.'

'Yes, Anna, I understand,' was all I could say. I wished we were somewhere else. The elderly woman across me, hair stiff with spray net and fingers on her black rosary beads, glared at us. An old man bared his teeth and gave us a lewd grin.

Anna's head was bowed so low I thought her head was like a flower that would just snap off from her neck shaped like a vase.

In silence, we got off in front of Stella Maris College. I flagged down a Golden Taxicab for Anna, mentally taking down its plate number. I wanted to comfort her, to offer her crumbs of words. Instead, all I did was wave goodbye. Inside the cab, sitting upright in that straight posture I would always associate with her, Anna's eyes seemed faraway, hidden by a wall of mist.

After her cab had turned left toward P. Tuazon, I walked on, dragging my green rubber shoes in the direction of the bookstore. Neon signs blinked their lies. Jeepneys farted their monoxide fumes.

And in the night sky drifted the sad moon.

Papa drove me to Anna's house for the Christmas party in our old, long car complete with tail fins. He had finished his two-year contract in Saudi Arabia and did not renew it. He opened a small store selling office supplies to nearby Camp Aguinaldo. Before we left the house in Antipolo, he gave me two bottles of *Davidoff Cool Water* for Christmas. One was an *eau de toilette*; the other was an aftershave. I told him I only asked for one but he said that was all right, since they were being sold at 50 per cent off.

Now, on the way to Blue Ridge, Papa was unusually quiet. His silent moments were rare, and they made me uncomfortable.

'Pa,' I began, 'what will you give me for my graduation? I want something that moves.'

'Bah, if you graduate with honours, I'll give this car to you! I'll even have it repainted and accessorized. Just for you. But if you merely graduate, well, perhaps a bicycle.'

I frowned at his attempt at humour. I wanted to tell him I did not want a gas-guzzler of a car, but I just smiled. Finally, I had passed Algebra last semester, after taking it for the second time. I was taking Business Statistics that semester. If I got a mark of at least a B, I thought, I would make it to Honourable Mention.

'We're here. No. 7 Hilltop Road, no?' He turned on the overhead light.

'Yes, Pa. Thanks. I might be home before one. I'll just hitch with one of my classmates.'

'Do you have enough money?'

Pa, just give me a hundred,' I said, a little embarrassed.

He flicked open the overhead light, groped for his brown imitation-leather wallet, then handed me two crisp hundred-peso bills. The soft yellow light drenched the grey-washed hair, the doe eyes that were also my eyes, the flab around the neck.

'Thanks again,' I muttered, kissed him on the cheek (smell of *Champion* cigarettes and *Tancho* pomade), then got off the car.

'Take care, son,' he called out to me, then turned off the overhead light. Since I turned twenty that year, my parents had allowed me to go to parties without the usual, irritating reminders about avoiding drugs and B.I. (bad influences). They must have gotten tired of suspecting me of doing things I would never even do, simply because everybody else was doing them. I had always wanted to be different.

Papa's words still echoed in my ears as I stood on the curb. A sudden gust of cold wind made me shiver. At the end of the road gleamed the rainbow lights of Marikina. I waited until the warm, familiar hum of our old car was gone. When I turned around, I saw Chito, a shadow between the two coconut trees. He startled me, so I said with a hint of annoyance: 'Have you been there long?'

'Your Dad and you are so sweet,' he said, smiling strangely. A whorl of smoke blurred his face, erasing his nose, eyes, his hair. For an instant, I thought he would just simply vanish.

'What's wrong with that?' I asked.

'Nothing, nothing really,' he answered, and then took a drag at his dope, which blazed like an eye in the darkness.

In silence, we entered Anna's house, with its tall brown steel gate and concrete walls that had turned dark-green with thick ivy. The house was split in three tiers, built to follow the curve of the hill slope.

Only half of the class attended the party. Our professor, who had required us to read *The Nuremberg Trials, Volumes I* and *II* for our class in Philosophy of Religion, was not around, either. I heard he had gone up to the mountain town of Sagada to read Gabriela Mistral, Pablo Neruda and Rainer Maria Rilke. Anna's parents were in Europe. Even without them, you could sense their presence in the very pores of the house. The four maids in white starched uniforms walked on their toes, as if afraid to stun the graceful fish in the white Ming plates and the long-legged birds in the porcelain vases. The cheerful Malang painting of the slums blended perfectly with the tawny wall carpet. On the library stood the mahogany shelves with their hardbound books of *The Guerilla Strategy in the Stock Market* and *Negotiable Instruments*. Their white Christmas tree reached to the ceiling, glittering with balls and baubles, stars and angels. Strips of gold and silver ran down the tree in graceful circles. Under the tree were many gifts in big boxes, wrapped in satin or woven abaca fibres.

Anna's brother, Rico, wore a blue Armani shirt and black jeans that hugged his thighs. He was drop-dead gorgeous. Much taller than Anna, he had one-inch long hair, sharp cheekbones and eyes that turned alternately brown and black with the light. He dazzled when he smiled, like a model in a toothpaste commercial. He had none of Anna's nervous energy, though. He did not mind serving our food (chicken barbecue, seafood paella, potato salad, *jamon de Serrano*). He also emceed our boisterous programme of song and dance, a job he obviously loved doing. But he was nowhere to be found later.

I had to get up every now and then to pee, because I had such weak kidneys. I had urinary-tract infection which, my doctor said, came from having too much salt in my food (must be all that fried fish and shrimp paste) and holding back my urine. I still got mad when my friends claimed it was an STD. How could I say it was not sexually transmitted, for that would mean admitting I was still a virgin at 20?

And I had also let go that night, drinking four bottles of beer and finishing a pack of *Marlboro*. My classmates were sprawled lazily on the rich, red carpet with curvilinear designs, amidst throw pillows covered in silk. We seemed to be floating on a cloud of smoke. I had to be careful not to step on my classmates. I could have peed in the toilet, or in the kitchen, which was nearer. But I had earlier discovered Anna's own little corner in the library, with its friendly books: *The Chronicles of Narnia*, the fairy tales of Oscar Wilde, Angela Carter's *The Bloody Chamber and Other Stories*.

The library was quite far, so my bladder was about to burst when I reached the door. I turned the knob, pushed the door open and froze.

In the half-light of the lamp Chito and Rico were sitting beside each other on the black leather couch. With tenderness, they were kissing each other's eyelids and lips, nuzzling earlobes and necks, their fingers caressing each other's bodies . . .

I just closed the door quietly.

The party broke up at around 2 a.m. Anna led us out of the house.

I didn't notice it had rained, which was rare in December. The road glistened, and all about us hung the pure, clean fragrance of newly washed leaves. Anna and I stood beneath the soft glow of the pagoda lanterns atop the big concrete posts.

'Bye, and thanks,' Anna said.

I said, 'Bye, Anna.' I could not help it, so I leaned closer to her. The punch she had drunk brought out the flush on her cheeks. 'Merry Christmas, Anna,' I whispered. 'Please don't be so sad.'

She broke into a thin, quick smile and kissed me back on the cheek.

Still Groovy After All These Years

A Feature Article

It must be the times we graduated because ours was not just a meeting for the sake of kissing each other's cheeks and noting who has gained 100 pounds in the last so many years. Oh yes, we did that, too, noting as well how the girls in my batch were getting younger and the boys seemed to be getting older so much quickly. The girls were beginning to land in the society pages of the Sunday newspaper supplements, having married well, in the Jane Austen sense, into this or that good family. And the boys, who used to be cute, were growing bellies and beginning to lose their hair.

We also met to raise funds for our educational projects: to help upgrade the level of teaching in the country's selected public schools. In effect, it meant teacher-training, book donating and gathering together our unused computers and giving them to the public schools, for them to be wired in this age when information came at the speed of light.

They also asked me to write something for our project's souvenir programme, around the line, 'Still Groovy After All These Years'. So I said our lives had always been groovy, if not nervy. After all, we started our university studies in 1979, when the president was bullshitting the country through his decrees and the First Lady was amassing 3,000 pairs of Italian shoes with such wild abandon. The elections for the National Assembly had just been rigged, with the fractious Opposition (the Opposition has always been fractious, in all countries, across the centuries) losing to the team of the First Lady and her obscure allies. But let us forget, in the meantime, the politicians. They would always stink, they would always be furry, they would always be there, like cockroaches. Only their faces would change, for son would take over the post of the father, and mother would warm the seat of the daughter, down the line of mongreldom.

Remember our classes? Mr B in physical education class who made me heft a barbell twice my weight of 90 pounds. Miss Y in Theology class who told us Jesus Christ would always carry our yoke for us. When she saw we were all sleepy (for it was three o' clock in the afternoon and her voice should be patented for it could surely cure insomnia), she asked: 'What does a yoke mean?' I raised my hand tentatively, she saw me, and I answered: 'Ma'am, the yellow part of an egg.'

Our History professor asked the most mind-boggling questions like, 'What was the height of national hero Doctor Jose P Rizal?' I was fortunate to remember Doctor Rizal's height. When I was in high school, we went on a field trip to Fort Santiago where Doctor Rizal was imprisoned before he was shot by musketry at Bagumbayan on a calm morning. I noted that Doctor Rizal was as tall as my mother, so I wrote the answer in my exam paper: 'Five feet, four inches tall.' Correct.

But then, the next question was, 'What was the name of Doctor Rizal's dog in Dapitan, where he was sent into exile by the Spanish authorities?' What the hell do I care? I thought to myself, at this volley of silly questions. But of course, I had to give an answer, and so I wrote, 'Bantay'. I could almost hear the buzzer in the quiz show on television going 'Ngeeeeee!' The correct answer was 'Usman'.

We also had a literature professor who was taught by Robert Penn Warren in the United States. When our professor was teaching us Lord Alfred Tennyson's poem, 'The Eagle', he stood on a chair, raised both hands as if they were wings, tucked his face out, and recited the whole poem from memory. I was fresh (fresh from the province of Pampanga and the *jeprox*, the rock 'n' roll boys of Project 4, Quezon City) and was surprised to see my professor looming in front of me, birdlike, his wide nostrils flaring such that I thought I could already see bits of his brain through his nose!

We also had a creative-writing professor who, when he was teaching us Rainier Maria Rilke's poem, 'The Spanish Dancer', turned on his cassette recorder to a tape of a Spanish flamenco music, picked up his castanets from his table, and began twirling and clacking the castanets round and round while reciting Rilke's immortal lines. Then he ended his passionate performance with a stomp of the foot and a crisp, *'Ole!'*

I could never do that, not in ten lifetimes.

We also had a History professor named Father Lenny, SJ, who would bring an armful of books and dump them on his table before the start of every class. He would then talk about historian Barbara Tuchman's books, *The Guns of August* and *The Proud Tower,* with such easy familiarity as if she just lived down the road. Then he added: 'When I am dead, these are the books I want to see on my chest.'

Father Lenny made boring history come alive before our eyes. He said: 'I was a young boy growing up in Maryland when I saw the footage of the Nazi occupation of Europe. Such cruelty you will never find elsewhere. That is why I cannot understand the *biblical* injunction about turning the other cheek, or giving a piece of bread to someone who has just cast a stone at you. Why, if a Nazi soldier cast a stone at me,' the priest added, his blue eyes widening and the veins on his temples beginning to throb, 'then, I would pick up a rock and throw it at him!'

Oh, we remember all of them, our professors cranky, weird and memorable, some of them beloved even, as we now move on into our lives as doctors and gentlemen farmers, businessmen and non-profit organisation workers, professors and jet-setters, stock brokers and real-estate brokers, politicians and socialites, homemakers and peacemakers.

Statistics from the placement office indicated that many of our batchmates were doing social-development work, breaking out of the mould that was hip and fashionable in the 1970s. We were educated by brilliant Jesuits with whisky on their breath. Our husbands and wives, boyfriends and girlfriends, did not love us all the time. We wished we were taller, slimmer, sexier, richer but at the back of our minds, we seemed to sense that, perhaps, this life is enough.

Our bones were not yet brittle and our teeth were not yet falling off. Our pores could still feel the coolness in the air. We could still sashay to *Dancing Queen* and jiggle to *Rock Lobster*. We could tell our children, both natural-born and adopted, our nephews and nieces, that our lives were not wasted after all.

You could even call us 'groovy' again (Jesus, that word is so 1970s.) Yes, I guess we are still groovy after all these years.

Victoria Station

M y cheeks were suddenly numb from the cold the moment I walked out of Gatwick Airport. After a fourteen-hour flight from Manila to London, I arrived at Gatwick at 4 a.m. There was none of Manila's boisterous airport crowd, where every overseas Filipino worker who leaves the country is sent off by a busload of family, relatives and friends. I still remember the scenes from yesterday, when a small boy just refused to let go of the hands of his mother who was going to work as a domestic helper in the Middle East. The mother's eyes had already turned red from crying but the young boy refused to let go. He just gripped his mother's hand and refused to cry. He just looked at her with his round and liquid eyes. I averted my gaze and instead arranged the things inside my bag.

The Customs man at Gatwick asked me, 'From Hong Kong?' and before I could answer that our Cathay Pacific plane just had a stopover there, he had already waved me aside. That saved me the task of unlocking the big, blue luggage that my father had given to me as a gift from Saudi Arabia. Then, I walked over to the foreign-exchange counter and exchanged my 100 US dollars for UK pounds, the big and crisp paper bills with the image of Queen Elizabeth in the centre. In front of me were two young Japanese girls in black mini-skirts and black stockings. I stole a glance at their traveller's cheques: thousands of pounds, my dear reader.

The airport's silence and the directions spelt in so many arrows could stump any Filipino out on his first overseas trip. A year ago, I had applied for a British Council Fellowship to study in the United Kingdom. The interview was done at their office in an old and elegant mansion in New Manila, with a white tower at the back and magnolias blooming like small suns in the garden. Mr Salmon, the British Council director, had asked me why I wanted to study English Literature in the UK.

'All these authors are dead, white men any way,' he said, a wicked twinkle in his eyes. 'So what is the point of reading them?' His eyes were the same colour as the soft shade of blue on the wallpaper behind him.

'Well, they may be dead, but their words live on. And anyway, the reading list now, I am quite sure, already includes live, female writers, as well as writers with different skin pigmentation and sexual orientations.'

'Quite true,' chimed in Mr Grant, the Cultural Affairs Officer, who would later become a friend of mine.

But the Brits were such cool cats, and they just laughed when I gave them my answer.

Mr Salmon said, 'Yes, indeed, Virginia Woolf is now part of the literary canon. But when I was reading English Literature at Oxford, she was not even part of the reading list. She was just considered a writer of *memoirs*.'

Mr Grant assented, adding that there was a young British novelist of Japanese descent, Kazuo Ishiguro, whom I should read. He added, 'That young man is a writer of such elegant and indirect prose. Who knows, he might win the Booker Prize one day?'

And Mr Salmon added, 'Or even the Nobel Prize for Literature as well?'

When I went out of the white and beautiful mansion I looked at the sky, which was as blue as the colour of my mother's elementary-school uniform, and thought that if I make it, I will miss this wide blue sky and my beautiful mother and the sweet-sour, vinegary-soy food of my country.

Naturally I got lost in the labyrinth of Gatwick Airport. I took a deep breath, walked to the nearest lift and pressed a button that brought me to the ground floor. Then I pulled my luggage and walked outside.

It was still dusk, a half-light suffused with muted tones of grey. It was only early spring, but a sudden clutch of coldness made me wear my winter coat in a huff. I saw a cleaning lady and asked her where I could get a ride to Victoria Station. She was polite and cheerful, her brown and curly hair bobbing as she moved her head as she spoke.

'Hello, sonny, just take the lift again to go up, turn right, and then there you are, at the train going to Victoria Station. The train runs every 15 minutes.'

I thanked her and then she chirped: 'I hope you will have a lovely holiday.'

The doors of the lift opened. Again I was faced with so many arrows. I saw a young woman in a cardigan abloom with the colours of autumn—red and orange and yellow, like leaves turning in the still air. I recognized her. She had boarded the plane at Hong Kong's Kai Tak Airport. I walked over to her and asked her how I could reach Victoria Station.

'Oh, I'm going there, too,' she said in a musical accent. 'You can come with me.'

The next ordeal was how to deal with the coins. How to count these coins that I am now just seeing for the first time? My friends in the Philippines had given me some UK pounds and coins before

I left, but I did not bother to familiarize myself with them. The train was already here and about to leave in a minute. How now, brown cow? But the young woman said it was fine, she dropped some coins in the turnstile for my fare, and she helped me pull my luggage as well. We reached the train just before the door shut and surprised a young couple who were deep in each other's embrace. The man smirked; the woman looked out of the window.

My new friend gave me her name, Fionnuala, and she talked with an accent that dipped and rose in the cold morning air. She worked as a banquet manager at a hotel in Seoul. 'Before I left, we had a farewell party, and the Filipinos who worked with me cooked so much food we had to bring home some of them. They even gave me gifts. They are so sweet.' She showed me one of her gifts, a round wooden key holder inscribed with the word 'Baguio', the name of this lovely mountain city in the north, where I broke my heart.

Outside, mist hung over the suburbs of London. Tall, sooty buildings made of bricks, then a blur of trees. 'I am Irish,' she said. 'I have an uncle who is a Catholic priest in Jeju Island off the mainland of Korea. I just visited him. It is a fantastic island.'

I smiled at her and glanced outside. The spires had become taller, the roads wider. We must be near London now, I thought. I looked back at Fionnuala, then fished out a green T'boli pendant (cool, clear depths) from my carry-on bag. 'May I give this to you, please?' I said. 'For your kindness.'

At first she did not want to accept it, but I told her I have a whole box of such pendants from the indigenous tribes to give away to people who were kind to strangers. She laughed and said, 'Oh you, Filipinos. You are such a lovely people.'

I was terribly hungry when we reached Victoria Station. Fionnuala and I bade goodbye to each other after the turnstile. The station was quiet and cavernous. I walked faster when I saw a food stall.

Instinct told me to ask for Sarsi and Skyflakes from the man at the counter. I stopped momentarily, shifting time zones, changing places, in my mind. When the gears had locked in place in my mind, I said, 'Could I have Coke and biscuits, please?'

The man's forehead furrowed. 'We have Coke but biscuits?'

I was hungry and did not want to think any more. 'Could I have those chocolates over there instead?' I pointed at the chocolate bars, counted my coins carefully, and then sat on a bench. Suddenly it was like a silent film by Charlie Chaplin, the men in pin-striped suits and the women in blue, well-cut dresses running after their trains. I just sat there, sipping my drink and munching at my chocolate bar, marvelling at how quickly I had been transported to another world so vastly different from mine.

I looked at my watch. Eight o' clock. The British Council office at Victoria Station must be open by now. I stood up, pulled my luggage and entered the British Council office. It was quiet, as usual. The man at the counter smiled at me, asked for my name, and then called the driver over. He was young, obviously a postgraduate student like me, working part-time to pay for his bills. He carried my luggage and deposited them at the boot of his car.

I opened the car's right door. 'Oooops, wrong side,' I said, when I saw the driver seated there. I walked to the other side and opened the door but I did not know how to strap the seat belt.

'Could you help me with this?' I asked the driver. He looked back and when I saw the unspoken question in his eyes, I said, 'Of course, we also have seat belts in my country. But we do not use them.' His jaw dropped. But he recovered quickly enough, smiled, and soon, our black car was nosing out of the garage.

The streets were wide, much wider than in Manila, and the people on the sidewalks walked fast. There was traffic but it moved. And nobody honked on their horn. When the driver saw through his mirror that I was looking at a big building, he said, 'Oh, that is the Buckingham Palace.'

I saw a grey building and so I asked, 'But where are the tulips? And the guards in red? I saw them in the postcards.'

He smiled. 'Perhaps in an hour the guards will be there,' he said, 'and the tulips, well, they are still bulbs now, but they will bloom in a few weeks.'

Soon we reached Trafalgar Square (flocks of pigeons, those elegant fountains) on whose centre stood Lord Nelson's monument. Finally, the van entered the garage of the British Council in Spring Gardens.

I thanked the driver, alighted, and then waited at the British Council office. I watched a stream of African students, postgraduate fellows like myself, walk into the building. Their clothes made of cotton always brought summer to my mind—bursts of iridescent colours, harbingers of light.

Then I stood up and asked the receptionist, 'Do you have a comfort room?'

'I'm sorry?' she said in an accent that I would later on learn was middle-class and South Londonish. In a clinical a way as possible, I explained to her what 'comfort room' meant, standing so upright even if my bladder was about to burst. 'Oh, you mean the *lah-vah-tree!*'

'Yes, indeed,' I said, and she politely gave me directions.

After I returned, I was ushered into the British Council office for my orientation. A woman with an assistant in tow ('she is training for the job, I hope you don't mind me bringing her along') handed me a sheaf of papers containing information on immigration matters, student visa renewal, monthly stipend—and a brochure on AIDS as well as several packets of condoms!

When the woman saw the shocked look in my eyes, she said, 'Oh, we give these to all of the British Council Fellows who study in the UK.' I was surprised because it was so difficult even to find condoms in conservative and Catholic Philippines during those times. And here, they were being given freely, available everywhere, like a chocolate drink or salt-free crackers in the vending machines.

I then went to the cashier, encashed my cheques and mapped out my plans for London in the next two days. I decided to return to my hotel to get some sleep. The woman who gave me the orientation and her assistant helped me put my luggage in the boot of the black cab.

'Where are you going, sonny?' asked the old driver. I wanted to say Gloucester Road, but I was too tired and worried I might pronounce it again incorrectly. So instead, I just gave him the sheet of paper with the address of the hotel. The black cab began to move. With its mostly white knuckles, London was rubbing the fog from its sleepy eyes.

Fifteen months to the day, when I was already back in Manila, an English friend would write me a letter. Angela apologized for 'what the British are doing to Iraq during the Gulf War'. Within a week, a rich student in the Philippine university where I taught would put a gun in his mouth and pull the trigger. His blood and brains would splatter on the white walls of their beautiful mansion in the suburbs. Another would be mauled to death by his fraternity brothers in a hazing ritual, first attaching electric rods to his balls and cranking up the battery, and then beating him up with wooden paddles until parts of his skin had turned completely black. And a bomb would explode right in the heart of Victoria Station, during the peak of the morning rush hour. Ten people would die. Hundreds would be wounded, would run screaming out of the tube on the cold ash-grey of morning.

Then I would put my knuckles to my eyes, rubbing them hard, wishing that this bombing would be the first and the last, and that everything was just a short nightmare.

A Brush with Royalty

It was spring and the birds were singing. I was living in a small room in a hotel run by Filipinos in Nevern Square, London. It was the break from the school term, and so I took a fourteen-hour train journey to visit London. That day I went to Saint Paul's Cathedral, its tall and beautiful spires reaching for the sky. I also finally saw the red tulips opening their smooth petals to the sun.

A crowd had gathered in front of the cathedral. The police were even there, in their red uniforms, carrying only their wooden sticks, unlike in the Philippines, where the policemen and the security guards carried long guns and a supply of bullets strapped to their waists. To my left, two Latin Americans were French-kissing. After six months here, I had been used to such public displays of affection. On the day I arrived, I was walking on Charing Cross Road, trying to look for number 84 where the famous book store was located, when I saw one, then two, then three couples kissing. I told myself, I better stop counting the number of people who kissed each other on the streets, you *barrio* boy.

Suddenly, the huge wooden doors of Saint Paul's Cathedral opened. Out came the archbishop of the Church of England, followed by people in finery, and finally, the Queen.

Queen Elizabeth walked down the stone stairs regally. She wore a lovely cream-coloured hat and an elegant pink suit. My only touchstone for royalty was still the First Lady of the Philippines, our queen who grew up in poverty before she married the young senator who would become the dictator of my country. Once, I saw the First Lady at the Cultural Centre of the Philippines, which she had built on reclaimed land near Manila Bay. On her arms coiled bracelets made of the brightest gold; the rings on her fingers shone with small fires more stunning than Joseph's amazing coat of dreams.

But here was the Queen of England, a former imperial power and owner of a world where the sun never set, wearing just a strand of pearls. A *single* strand of pearls. She did not have to project anything: her breeding exuded from her, like fragrance rising from her skin.

The people just clapped politely but the two Latin Americans beside me broke away from their fierce embrace. I folded the small map of London I had been studying. And then the three of us, as if on cue, began waving. Not only that, we also squealed with delight as Queen Elizabeth passed before us. We must have startled her because her head jerked perceptibly, then her smile widened at us, the Latin Americans and this Latin Asian, the flamboyant Latino vibe in our souls.

But when I told this incident to my Irish and Scottish friends in the smoky Barnton Bistro pub a fortnight later, they refused to comment. Their silence had the coldness and clarity of ice. They refused to comment and just looked away, drank their Guinness, and smoked their fags. And then their talk shifted to Prime Minister Margaret Thatcher, the Iron Lady whom they hated with passion. They even invited me to attend a protest rally against her to be held in Edinburgh at the end of the month. They were protesting against the steep increase in school fees and the plan to cut the subsidy for the National Health Service. I told them that I would just help them make colourful protest banners and pithy placards, which are the specialities of the rabble-rousing Filipinos.

But aside from this uncomfortable silence when I mentioned the name of the Queen, my classmates were generally friendly. When winter set in, announced by a chill that hung in the air for months, I followed all their suggestions to fend off the horrible cold. I wore woollen long johns and several layers of clothes, thick gloves and a bright blue bonnet that made my classmates smile. Then, I draped myself with my thick, yellow overcoat, an expensive Gucci overcoat that was lent to me by a rich Chinese Filipino friend. When I first wore it my classmates laughed, saying that people 'ovah there' dressed according to the weather. Cotton and flower-printed textiles in summer, orange and red aflame in autumn, and then the colour tones muted in winter: grey and black overcoats, with the dash of colour coming from a scarf made of wool.

But I answered, 'Don't you want to see a spot of sun, a bright blob, walking on campus in the midst of all this British gloom?'

They would just smile and laugh, my bright and friendly cohort. I continued going out with them to Barnton Bistro. Every night, we drank and talked endlessly until the last calls for drinks were announced at ten minutes to midnight. Until the Christmas break came, I was sampling every kind of drink offered in the bar. I liked it so much that one day, I wrote to my father that 'I had discovered the many pleasures of drinking here'. But my father, who could be roaring drunk at times, simply ignored my letter.

I just went ahead and drank—whiskey distilled and bottled in Scotland, red wines from the finest vineyards of France, and that old reliable, Guinness Beer, truly dark and truly potent, made in the breweries of Ireland. I needed to fortify myself from the arctic wind that blasted at me the moment I stepped out of Barnton Bistro to hail a cab that would bring me back to the university.

One time, a Filipino friend of mine visited and we ate at Barnton Bistro. We were waiting for a cab and talking in Tagalog when two punks with their girlfriends began imitating the way we spoke. One of them then said: 'You bitter go beck to China.'

I eyed him and I said, 'We're *not* from China.'

'Then where the hell arrre you frrrom? Ye should just go beck home.'

But before I could go to them and answer, an older gentleman approached them and told them off. He then walked over to us and apologized. 'I am sorry about this. We rarely have them here. But I recognize your accent very well indeed. Are you Filipinos? My daughter is married to a Filipino and they live in Toronto. He is such a kind fellow. My daughter loves him so.'

He spoke quickly and passionately, his grey eyes profuse with apology. 'It is all right, sir,' I said. Then we shook each other's hand before he said farewell and left. I bought my friend newly cooked fish and chips to comfort him, delicious and hot with a dash of vinegar.

One night, we decided to have a Christmas party in Desmond's house, an Irish guy who teased my American English on the first day of class when I called him 'my seat mate'. After studying in Dublin, Desmond received a scholarship grant to take up Actuarial Science at Georgetown University in Washington, D.C. He said the cavernous Immaculate Conception Church was always filled with Filipinos, Latinos and Irish every Sunday. Afterward, he went to the University of Stirling in Scotland to take a postgraduate degree in English Literature.

Desmond was quiet, good-looking and bright. There was also a sadness about him that I could not place. I liked him immediately. Before I left for the United Kingdom, my mother told me there were two things I should not forget to do in Scotland—to study hard because I represent my country and it would be such an embarrassment to land at the bottom of the class, and to attend the Holy Mass every Sunday. Desmond lived a mile away from the university and every Sunday, I saw him in the university chapel. We sat beside each other during the Holy Mass, listening with rapt attention to the booming voice of the young, robust priest from South Africa.

One day, Desmond invited me to have lunch in his flat. We walked in the cool, bracing air of autumn. The maple leaves were already turning into the colour of fire. He said he had prepared something for lunch, something Irish: 'hamburgers and boiled potatoes'. And so we ate the char-broiled hamburgers and soft, boiled potatoes that he had prepared for lunch.

'For dessert,' he said, 'I bought you something that you must be missing by now.' He bent down and from under the dining table and retrieved a coconut. Not a young one, with fresh coconut water and meat so soft it melts in your mouth. It was an old and brown coconut, whose tough meat could already be used for copra.

I smiled and said politely, 'Your coconut seems a bit old and tough for dessert.'

'So I got the wrong one?' he asked and then smiled sheepishly.

But you have to give him 20 points for effort and generosity. We always held parties in his house and we decided to hold our Christmas party there. My classmates went ahead to his house. It was already dark when Desmond and I set out from the university. Fog floated before us. The tall birch trees had no more leaves, and the branches looked like wraiths in the icy air. Our boots trudged on the freshly fallen snow, all of one foot thick, and quite slippery such that we had to walk carefully.

When we arrived at Desmond's house, we immediately ate the seafood pizza and drank the soda as well as the gin & tonic that our classmates had prepared. There was a new singer named Sinead

O' Connor and when my classmates played her hit song, *Nothing Compares 2 U,* everybody stood up to dance. In the darkened living room, the boys danced with the girls, while two girls danced with each other. I just sat in the corner, arms akimbo, certainly feeling like Nora Ephron's wallflower in the orgy. Just then, someone in the shadows came to me. It was Desmond and he was asking me to dance with him. At first I was confused, but since I was easily swayed, I stood up to dance with him. But Desmond was just cool about the whole thing. I was not even sure if he was bisexual, gay or, as they now say it now in the gay dating apps, bi-curious. He just embraced me and we danced wordlessly even if my heart was booming in my chest. It was my first time to dance with another man and I felt my body shivering. Desmond must have noticed it so he just embraced me tighter. His body was so warm. The music was so loud and he was saying something. His breath smelt of whiskey and I wanted to believe that he was saying that he liked me, although it might be because I was already hard of hearing, even if I was only 26: either hard of hearing or simply filled with a hopeless fantasy that Desmond was besotted with me.

After the party, which we all agreed was a smash, I helped tidy up Desmond's house and then he brought me back to my flat in the university dormitory. It was already 1 a.m., and there was neither bus nor cab in sight. The snow was falling again in thick and endless flurries. The polar wind was beginning to rise, making a sound like that of someone keening in the night. And my cheeks were turning numb again.

Then Desmond said gently, 'Just ignore the cold and walk on.'

It's because you are from Ireland, I wanted to say, where snow was general and fell faintly through the universe and faintly fell, from church spire to mountain top to the grey Irish Sea. But I just walked beside him quietly, in that landscape of snow, until we saw the warm glow of light coming from my flat at Muirhead Hall.

The Foreign Student

B eing a foreign student in the United Kingdom meant living on the proverbial shoestring. Along with the Malaysian and Singaporean students in Muirhead Hall, I went to the supermarket on our first day to make our most important acquisition—our rice cooker. With this precious acquisition, we could cook our soft and fragrant rice, unlike the hard rice that passed for cooked rice in the cafeteria. We could also steam our vegetables, cook our stewed pork and prepare assorted viands of chicken and beef that would make our South East Asian palates happy.

I also liked going once a week to the meat section in the supermarket. Billy, the kindly old Scot manning the section, always set aside pork lungs and heart for me. He would wrap them in several layers of blue plastic and hand them to me with a smile. This, after I had ordered my week's supply of minced meat, chicken wings and bishop's nose (chicken ass), the cheapest kinds of meat that I could find.

After I had put the meat in the freezer, I would proceed to cook *bopis*, a spicy Filipino dish made from the minced lungs and heart of a pig. It can be served as an appetizer for beer and alcohol; it is also considered a main dish and is best served with steamed white rice. It certainly fortified me and made me happy in my twelve months of genteel poverty in merry, olde Scotland.

How to cook *bopis*? It is important to neutralize the pungent and gamy odour of the pig's lungs before starting to cook. There are different ways to do this. One is to boil and simmer the lungs with cooking wine; the other is to boil them with several sticks of lemon grass.

Bopis

INGREDIENTS

1 1/2 lbs pig's lungs boiled in lemon grass
1 lb pig's heart boiled in lemon grass
1/2 cup annatto seeds diluted in 1 cup of water
1 small carrot, minced
6 tablespoons white vinegar
2 tablespoons bird's eye chili, minced
2 tablespoons ginger, minced
1 medium onion, chopped
4 cloves garlic, minced
4 pieces dried bay leaves
1 cup water
3 tablespoons cooking oil
Salt and pepper to taste

Instructions

1. Heat a frying pan or wok and pour the cooking oil.
2. Sauté ginger, garlic and onion.
3. Add the bird's eye chili and cook for around one minute.
4. Put the minced pig's lungs and heart, then cook for five minutes while stirring occasionally.

5. Pour the annatto water from the diluted annatto seeds and stir.
6. Add the dried bay leaves and pour 1 cup of water. Simmer for 40 minutes or until almost all the liquid has evaporated.
7. Add the minced carrots and stir. Simmer for around five minutes.
8. Season with salt and ground black pepper, then stir.
9. Pour the vinegar and cook for 10 minutes on medium heat.
10. Turn off heat and transfer to a serving plate.

Bopis saved me a lot of money; I always ate it at least twice a week. But on the third month, I went to the supermarket again and Billy asked me about my dog.

'How is yerrrr dog?' he enquired.

'What dog?' I answered.

'The one that you feed with the pig's lungs and heart that I set aside for you everrry week.'

I was momentarily stunned.

Then I said, recovering quickly: 'Oh, *my dog*. Yes, my dog, Spot. He is *very*, *very* healthy. Thanks to your pig's lungs and heart.'

He grinned from ear to ear, happy that he was helping feed my dog. And then he gave me another blue plastic bag containing my provisions for a week's worth of bopis.

Green Roses

Spring. Even then, a piercing chill in the air.

Past Queen's Park with its dark trees I walked. On the other street, the lamp post stood tall and sooty in front of Robert Louis Stevenson's flat. Lamplight froze on the cobblestones. The arctic wind gusted.

Down I walked. The shops had all been boarded up and closed promptly at five o clock on a Saturday afternoon. It had been six hours since then. Now yuppies in their grey Volvos drove past, their dates wearing red dresses, on their way to the cafes. Far ahead, at the street's end, the spires of Edinburgh were black points against the sky.

Green Roses, said the neon sign atop the doorway. The green petals were luminous in the night.

'Evenin', son,' said the fat bouncer, his woollen sweater beginning to pill, the lint ravelling.

'Hi,' I said. I was sure he did not recognize me, although I had been in the bar just a fortnight ago. I went there with the university's Gay Society members.

That was my first time in a bar. I went along with them simply because I had wanted to. No grand declarations of liberation, the way they do it in American films. I had just finished reading

Edmund White's novel, *A Boy's Own Story*. After reading the book, I just felt a glass window sliding open, and the horizon suddenly in front of me had no more boundary, a calm blue sea that just went on and on. I was tired of shuttered rooms.

The bar was clean. There were two screaming queens and the rest were straight-acting lads: your jolly bus driver, your friendly doctor at the National Health Service, your local soccer hero. It was a Thursday night and the place was hardly full.

'Can I buy you a drink?' asked Robert, the Gay Society president. Robert was tall and blonde and skinny. We called him Twiggy. I had known him for one academic term and I knew that his offer meant only that—a harmless drink.

'Yes, thanks,' I answered with a smile. Then I turned to the bar boy: 'One gin & tonic, please.'

The bar boy was gorgeous. He looked like Matthew Broderick and he seemed to know it. Our eyes locked, but only briefly. He fixed me a drink. With my friends, I sat on a couch with its soft skin of leather.

After finishing my drink, I walked to the lavatory. I was pissing when a potbellied man stood beside me, unzipped his trousers and began pissing as well. 'Are you a Chink?' he asked, then looked swiftly at my cock.

I was afraid but I did not want to show it. 'No,' I said. 'I'm from Thailand.'

'What's your name?'

'Porntip,' I said, 'Porntip Nakhirunkanok,' giving him the name of Miss Thailand who had won the Miss Universe beauty pageant.

'Ahhh—' he said, still trying to decipher my name, whose many syllables were already vanishing in the cold air.

'I have to go. I have company outside,' I said.

In a flash I was gone.

That was a fortnight ago. Now I was there again, making a go of it, alone.

When I stepped down the ScotRail at the station in Edinburgh and hailed a black cab, I felt a thrill run through me. It was the thrill of being a nobody in another country, the delicious thrill of anonymity. If only shadows could feel, I thought, perhaps this was how they would feel.

Saturday night had just begun but the place was already full. Faces always swung to the entrance the moment the black door opened. Eyes roved from your face down to your pecs, your crotch, your thighs.

I looked around. There was nobody I knew. No friend from the Gay Society this time to provide me with company. I just walked straight to the bar.

I ordered the same drink, the gin & tonic that I had before. The gorgeous bar boy was not there.

To my left, a man was looking me over. I turned to him, fullface. He looked like my mad uncle, the one who called himself 'a Roman Catholic to the bone'.

'Have I seen you before?' he asked in a thick brogue.

'I'm afraid not.'

His face cracked into a smile. 'How do you find this city?'

I paid for my drink. 'Lovely,' I said, 'but cold.'

'Ahhhh—,' he said, his *ahhh* floating in the air like hopeful balloons.

I scanned the bar, looking for an empty seat.

'Errr—perhaps what you need is human warmth?' he said finally, pressing my thigh.

'Yes,' I said, 'I think you're right.'

I took his hand off my thigh. With long strides I crossed the bar and sat in the corner.

The table beside me had copies of *The Pink Paper*. Back at the university, the Gay Society members and I would leave copies of the free weekly paper in Robbins Hall, the main building. In a few minutes, all the copies would be gone. But only around ten people dared to sign up when the Gay Society issued a call for new members. I was one of these newbies.

The night was getting warmer. The temperature of the crowd was rising as well. Any moment now, the dance floor downstairs would open. I picked up the latest issue of *Gay Times*, with Hanif Kureishi on the cover. I loved his *My Beautiful Laundrette,* which I had seen in Manila. My friend, the writer Jessica Zafra, had insisted that I watch the film before I flew to London.

I watched it in the living room of our house when I thought everybody had already fallen asleep. Just when Johnny, the punk played by Daniel Day-Lewis was beginning to kiss Omar, his Pakistani boyfriend played by Gordon Warnecke, my grandmother just burst suddenly into the living room like an Angel of Vengeance. But more like a tired, old angel, really, in her loose, floral house dress. I was surprised at her appearance. I just told her I was watching the film for a term paper I was writing at the university, then I pressed the remote control to fast-forward. The images on the television screen blurred. I was not even sure she saw the television screen, with her bad eyesight. She just gave me a pained look (perhaps her arthritis was bothering her again). Without saying anything, she just went to the lavatory.

Of course, when she had gone back to the room, it was flashback time again at the remote control, then freeze. It was my first time to see two men kissing each other with such passion and urgency, and perhaps the beginning of love.

But now, somebody sat from across me. I looked up. Oh dear, another train wreck. A caterpillar moustache.

'Errr, wherrrre ye from?'

'The Philippines.'

'Wherrrre is det?'

'Near Hong Kong.'

'Ye speak verrry good English.'

'I learnt it from my parents.'

'Who taught English to yer parents?'

'The missionaries.'

'And what happened to the missionaries?'

'My parents ate them.'

He moved away.

Before another inquisitor could ask me where I learnt my English, I already stood up. Just in time, for the green light atop the door leading to the dance floor below began to blink. It was time to jive.

I began walking to the door.

Soft grey smoke. Strobes spilling light. I ordered my second gin & tonic. Gorgeous was at the bar now. He fixed my drink. I was a bit sore because he did not recognize me, even if I wore the same gear a fortnight ago: long-sleeved black silk shirt tucked into tight, black jeans.

I stood in a corner, under a blown-up black-&-white photograph of James Dean. His sad and beautiful face was almost lost in the collar of his black, leather jacket. His hands were deep in his pockets and in the rain he walked, shoulders hunched against the cold.

Couples began moving to the floor. The young lads danced with such wild abandon. Their arms whirled in the air, golden hair tossing about, limbs long and electric. One boy wore tighter-than-tight black cycling shorts that showcased the silhouette of his family jewels. Another wore faded jeans ripped in appropriate places.

Two lovely lasses held hands while they danced, their long hair swinging. One of them was open-faced, like a beautiful flower. The other had violet fingernails and the reddest of lipsticks.

Angela Carter would have called her mouth a sensuous wound. They were both tall and stunning in their leather minis.

A man in his forties danced with another man of almost the same age range. They were both fat and their bodies were beginning to sag. They danced badly, out of rhythm. In fact, to no rhythm at all. But they must be lovers, I thought. Their eyes spoke only to each other.

I have the power – BOOM! BOOM! – I have the power, blared the invisible speakers. I finished my drink, stepped over on the gleaming dance floor, moved to the centre and began to dance. Smoke floated from the fog machine. Laser lights of many colours pierced me suddenly, beautifully. I threw my head back: the globe hanging from the ceiling caught my face and mirrored it in a thousand fragments of glass.

Then I saw him.

Shirt, leather jacket, jeans, boots, all in cool, sexy black. I looked away. When I looked back, he was still there, watching me. Faster and faster the song spun, the dancers' bodies and mine gyrating, swinging, the room burning, turning into a rectangle of fire.

The song ended. I went back to my seat in the corner. He drew nearer to me.

'Hello,' he said in a bright and cheerful voice. 'My name is Angus.' He had full lips, high cheekbones, eyes smiling but sad. His blonde hair was trimmed close to his scalp. A gold stud gleamed on his left ear.

'Hi,' I told him my real name. 'Nice ring,' I added, looking at his Celtic ring.

'My grandmother from the Orkney Islands gave it to me.'

I smiled. 'Come on, let's dance.'

We moved over to the dance floor. He danced well. Light fell on his smooth and beautiful face. Smoke slithered on the floor, caressing his thighs. Imagine what those thighs can do to you, I thought as I smiled at him. Blood pounded in my temples as the song turned faster and faster. He spun around once. Nice ass, tight as a drum. Sweat poured down my back.

After dancing to two more songs, we went up. He bought two pints of Guinness. There were other men around us talking, or posing, or nursing their nth drinks.

We sat on the bar stools. Angus said he had dropped out of the university.

I bought another round of Guinness.

'We're three boys in the family,' he said, suddenly cupping my hands in his hands. 'One day, my mother just suddenly asked, out of nowhere, if I were gay. "Yes," I said. "That's all right then," she said. "Your father and I won't love you less because of that."'

I smiled tightly. Yes. Home, which for me is a like a ship anchored on a misty harbour. You could glimpse its outlines; you know it is there. But its pure solidity you cannot touch, lost as it is amidst the grey and the vapour.

He drew my face closer to his face. Lovely cloud of Guinness on his lips. The first notes of a song floated in the air.

'Must be Sinead O' Connor's *Nothing Compares 2 U*?' I said. I wanted to ask him to dance. I remembered that my classmate Desmond and I had danced to that song a month ago. I liked Desmond, my sad Irish boy. I knew he also liked me but he told me later that he was just getting over a heartbreak. He said he was not yet ready for a new relationship.

We waited. Not Sinead. Wrong song. We both laughed. Then Angus looked at me, his eyes the colour of far mountains. His left hand touched the back of my head, drawing me closer to him. He closed his eyes and then he embraced me tightly. His eyelashes were softly curved and golden. He gave me swift, soft kisses on the lips. Then very long, very slow kisses. He ran his fingertip down my back. Lightly, lightly, as if my silk shirt were water. I shivered, goose bumps abloom on my skin. I opened my mouth and our tongues fused together, like the spirals in his Celtic ring.

And in my mind, the images began to burn. He will not touch me with his fingers, but with his fingertips. He will not caress my skin, but the hair on my skin. He will bathe me with kisses from forehead to thighs, then he will blow on my skin. The combination of coldness and heat will be potent. My pores will open suddenly, beautifully. Inside me a nerve ending, or something, will snap. His tongue will swirl in my earlobes, down to my nipples and my navel. The shocks of delight will send my body tingling. Round and round, pools of such incredible heat, then faster, my body rising like a hill, rising to meet him: sky exploding in a million fireworks of light.

Then I thought of the two middle-aged men downstairs, the ones whose eyes had a language of their own.

His hand in mine, we left the bar.

The chilly air made us shiver the moment we opened the door. The air smelt faintly of the sea, the salty tang borne by the wind blowing in from the Firth of Forth. The grand Georgian buildings of Edinburgh were still deep in shadows. Between the buildings, the alternating light and darkness had turned the cobblestones into chessboards.

I looked back. *Green Roses*. No, not the green colour of moss, melancholy and moist. More like the green crispness of young apples. The raw and startling smell of spring.

We walked close together, my man and I, to our cab.

Fear of Flying

ut such fantasies never came to fruition. When Angus and I
B arrived at his flat, which was located far away from swanky
Morningside in Edinburgh, he wanted us to drink more liquor. He
mixed vodka tonics and we drank several rounds until his speech
began to slur.

'I think we should sleep now,' I said, still excited at the prospect
of sleeping with this gorgeous young man.

'You bet . . . we should,' he said, lapsing into an Americanism
that alarmed me. The young man from the Orkney Islands stood
up and went to the loo to pee. When he came back, he turned off
the lights and lay down on one side of the bed.

I was torn between sleep and desire, between Scylla and
Charybdis, between now and forevermore. 'Angus,' I called for him
and he turned to face me. He parted his lips that were slightly askew.
The fumes from all the liquor he had drunk blasted before me.

Then he opened his eyes. His eyes were glazed with the liquor
and he kissed me on the mouth. I tasted vodka and gin and I shut
my eyes. This better be good, I told myself, since I have waited for
this all my life.

Angus took off his clothes and I took off mine and we threw
them in lumps on the floor. Then we kissed again and we touched

each other's bodies, hurried and hungry caresses, but then . . . but then he could not get it up. Instead of the hard and mighty Wallace Monument, all I touched was an earthworm, soft and small and sheathed in its skin. I used the weapons in my arsenal—fingers and mouth and breath and all—but it just remained what it was, a ghost of its former self, a simulacrum of what could have been. And then Angus turned his back to me and fell asleep. Pretty soon, he was snoring and had tumbled over, inevitably, on to the ravine of Never-Never Land.

So instead of the sparks I thought I would see when I first made love with someone I like, all I touched was an earthworm, all I heard were snores, and all I saw was a back turned to me in that cold and lonely bed.

I was pissed for a few minutes, but sleep also began to take its toll. Before I finally fell asleep, I remembered Soup Number 5, a dish that my father and his male friends in the military air base would cook. I would sometimes eavesdrop in their conversations in the late afternoons as they cooked Soup Number 5 and the viands of goat meat in our back yard.

The soup was supposed to have aphrodisiac qualities. It was usually consumed along with vast amounts of alcohol. The soup was supposed to balance the effects of the alcohol, like yin and yang, holster and gun.

Soup Number 5

INGREDIENTS

4 tablespoons chopped garlic
6 tablespoons minced tamarind
1 whole cow's penis and testicles, cleaned very well indeed
8 cups water

6 tablespoons chopped onions
1 tablespoon whole peppercorns
1 beef bouillon cube
2 tablespoons chopped spring onions
Fish sauce to taste

1. Sauté garlic in cooking oil until golden brown. Set aside.
2. Boil the tamarind in water then mash, strain, and set the juice aside.
3. Boil the cow's organs in water and then scrape with a knife to further clean them.
4. Bring water to a boil in a large pot. Add the meat and a pinch of salt. Simmer until tender.
5. Remove the meat from the broth and cut into cubes.
6. In a pan, heat the oil, then sauté the onions and cubed meat. Add the broth, peppercorns, and beef bouillon. Bring to a boil.
7. Add the tamarind juice, spring onions, and fried garlic. Season with fish sauce.

Hot, sour, and lovely, Soup Number 5 could certainly perk up all kinds of appetites, especially the only one that mattered most to me that unfortunate night in Edinburgh. I just hoped that I had Soup Number 5 for Angus that night, to bring him back to me from the icy depths of the Arctic Sea.

Home

Summer was just beginning and I returned to Manila on the dot, as soon as my British Council Scholarship was finished. I did not even entertain any thoughts of being an undocumented alien like some of the Filipinos I had met in the UK. Within a second after meeting them, they would whisper to me about this job opening or that opportunity. And when I answer I would come home after my grant, their eyes would widen, their mouths turning into the letter O.

I also returned to attend our class reunion, which was held three months after I returned to Manila. I would see them again after five years, my classmates who had organized the reunion, which I had thought silly because it was so early. But they had insisted: maybe they wanted to keep track of each other's direction, or lack of it. The humanities and literature majors seemed to have fanned out in all imaginable places, while the business majors in our cohort were working at the Makati Central Business District, or getting that MBA at Wharton or Harvard, then off to Wall Street, coolly earning their fat salaries and bonuses.

I would see them again after five years. What words would I offer to my dear classmates, Chito and Anna? Had new layers of skin grown over the old?

Chito and I began to drift away from each other after our Christmas party. He did not even know that I had already flown to London for my postgraduate studies. When we met on campus, we only nodded to each other, or jerked our eyebrows up in greeting. He had followed the template his father had prepared for him—he was now in Law School and doing rather well. And later, marriage, two kids healthy enough to endorse an advert for milk on TV, a mansion in Ayala Alabang, with a garage for at least three SUVs?

Last I heard, Anna was writing for a small publishing house that puts out children's books, much to the irritation of her mother, who wanted to train her in running the big family corporation that Anna would inherit. But Anna had declared her independence, was now living away from home, surviving on a meagre writer's pay, and perhaps writing, deep into the night, The Great Filipino Children's Novel.

And, yes, what about me?

I was still looking for somebody to live with, somebody who would watch films with me, talk to me with intelligence and wit, hold my hand when the waves of sadness threaten to drown me suddenly, inexplicably. Luis was gone and so was Mario. Angus came and went like one of the four seasons in Scotland—quickly, inevitably, the poor sod. I just know that one day, someone will come to me, bearing gifts of gladness and of grief.

I still went to the Holy Mass when I could, especially when someone I knew had died, in which case, I really had to attend the Holy Mass simply because that person's wake would be held in church. I still went to the Holy Mass, although at times, God seemed colder than the sea water in Morong, Bataan, where I taught English as a second language part-time to the children of Vietnamese refugees at the, uh, Bataan Processing Centre. As if the memories of a fatal war could be blurred by teaching them how to shop at J.C. Penney or open a checking account at the Bank of America.

But when I saw my students, their young faces golden in the morning sun, I remembered Chito and Anna.

One night when I returned from the Bataan Processing Centre, our apartment seemed to have become both familiar and strange, like a book I had not read in a long time. After coming back from Scotland, I had wanted to be as far away as possible from my family: they always asked me interminable questions why I came home late. So I signed up to teach three days a week in Bataan, helping the refugees who took rickety boats and crossed an ocean to flee from a horrible war. I wanted nothing else but solitude and space. I fixed my own food, washed my own dishes, did my own laundry, and cleaned my own room. I wanted my own personal space.

I was home that summer, and after the usual heavy dinner of beef *caldereta* cooked in spicy tomato sauce, the meat so soft it almost melted in my mouth, I went to the kitchen, out of habit, to wash the dishes. Mama was surprised, my father laughed, and my grandmother just smiled, adrift on the barge of her dreams. Ludy, the now-fat Ludy, washed the dishes. I noticed my diplomas and graduation photographs in their wooden frames, still hanging on the walls whose blue paint had begun to flake off in parts, especially near the ceiling. I stepped out of the house and on to the front yard, whose leaves gathered around me like an embrace. I thought of the past, the present and the future, images stretched out before me like the cars in a long, locomotive ride.

I thought of the flash from the photographer's camera catching me with my head tilted to the left, my wide eyes wanting to contain the universe within my eyelashes; my father rushing every morning to go to work, then rushing every afternoon to travel 30 miles away to take up a university course for four years, and on to Law School for another four years; my mother teaching her students to sing

'Auld Lang Syne', her voice a solid soprano vibrating like a laser of light in the air; the military airbase like a scoop of land between the plains of Floridablanca and the mountains of Zambales, an infinity of images like old, grainy photographs; Luis and the sadness of not telling him how I felt for him, the silk of his skin like the sheen of that river where he swam many years ago; of Roxanne with the lips red as strawberries on the mountain city shrouded with fog; of the unutterable words that lay frozen on my tongue as I spoke to Mario whom I loved, both of us sitting beside the fountain in the chilly air; of the city exploding with its incredible noises and colours, Ali Mall and Fiesta Carnival and the amorous love in the darkness of the cinema houses; of the university sitting on top of a hill, *Lux in Domino*, a shining sword raised to the bluest of sky; of Desmond from Ireland of the greenest mountains and Angus from the faraway Orkney Islands, one love unrequited and the other unconsummated, such ill luck I have; of my beautiful country governed by crocodiles and vipers, may they all rest in peace; of my love for words, like candle-flame cupped by my hands against wind and water; the many stories that still need to be told, the images flowing from the very heart of memory . . .

For a moment, though, as I stood there in our backyard, between our lighted house and the darkness beyond, there was neither sadness nor fear, only the humming of the cicadas, a humming so clear and alive.

Stirling-London-Cambridge-Los Angeles-Manila
1 January 2015